ARSONIST

a thriller

VICTOR METHOS

The mind is its own place, and in itself can make a heaven of hell, a hell of heaven.

— John Milton, *Paradise Lost*

Clover Middle School, San Diego, California. Eleven years ago.

The corpse swung lazily from the rope around its neck.

Thirteen-year-old Michael Haley stepped out of his classroom and was the first to see the body. He didn't recognize it for what it was at first, and thought that maybe some balloons were loose in the hallway of Clover Middle School. Then the general shape became clear.

The cat had been gutted, and its entrails spilt over the linoleum of the hallway. As the classrooms emptied into the corridor, Morgan Hollander slipped on some of the organs and fell, blood dripping on her from the corpse. Michael heard laughter from down the hall.

A boy stood near the exit, doubled over in laughter so hysterical that he looked as though he might fall over and not be able to get back up.

"Dude," Jesse said as he came up behind Michael. "What the hell?"

"It's that freak," Michael said, not taking his eyes off the laughing figure at the end of the hall.

"I know that guy. His name's Nehor."

Since he considered himself her boyfriend, Michael walked over and helped her to her feet. Her blonde hair and clothes, always the most expensive clothes in school, were dotted with crimson.

She started crying. "Look at my clothes."

"The blood will come out."

"Blood?"

Michael realized she hadn't seen the cat hanging above her. He tried to hurry her into a room, but Morgan saw everyone else looking up, and her eyes were drawn upwards, as well.

She screamed so loudly that it hurt Michael's ears. He looked down the hall and saw Nehor on the ground, his legs curled up to his chest, still laughing so much he was choking.

"Fuck that kid!" Michael sprinted for him.

Jesse followed, calling out to get a few more boys to join them. Nehor saw them coming, leapt to his feet, and ran outside.

The sky was gray and overcast as Michael sprinted out of the building and jumped down the ramp into the school parking lot. He spotted Nehor running across the soccer field, which was enclosed with thick shrubbery. Beyond that, a small forest led to the mansions of Atlas Peak Road. Nehor ran for a hole in the shrubs that had been cut long before he ever came to the school.

Michael reached the hole and looked over his shoulder. At least six or seven other boys were following. That freak had gotten away with too much for too long. Nehor had once come to school naked, and when the teacher led him out of the room, he peed all over the floor and desks on the way out. He was suspended for a month, and when he got back, Michael beat him until he was unconscious. Michael had kicked his ass so many times over the past two years that it had gotten boring. It had been a while since the last fight, but Nehor had messed with his girl, so Michael had to teach him a lesson.

Michael dove into the hole and ran through the forest. The trees were tall, and leaves covered the ground, crunching under his feet as he ran.

A small ditch lay ahead, and Michael slowed down to make sure he didn't trip on anything. Suddenly, he felt an explosion on the back of his head and saw a white flash as he fell headfirst into the ditch. When he rolled over, Nehor was standing a few feet away holding a thick branch. He was laughing again.

Michael struggled to his knees. Nehor swung and slammed the wood into Michael's jaw. His laughter changed to a high-pitched giggle.

Michael bent down and tried to catch his breath. He was dizzy, and his face hurt. "You freak! I'm gonna fucking kill you."

Nehor took off his backpack and unzipped it. He pulled out a bottle labeled Lighter Fluid.

Nehor tilted the bottle and squeezed. A stream of liquid arced through the air toward Michael's face. Michael yelled, and some of the fluid ran into his mouth. He began to cough, but the fluid didn't stop. It ran down his back and over his pants and shoes. It soaked his neck and chest. Anger turned to fear when he couldn't suck in any air and his lungs tightened. He looked up and saw Nehor standing over him.

Nehor lit a match, calmly letting the flame come down to his fingers and burn them. Michael began to cry. He couldn't feel the tears because the lighter fluid had made his face slick and numb.

Nehor started to laugh again. He lit another match, held it high, and danced around in a circle. He came up behind Michael and shouted, "Boo!"

Michael jumped, and Nehor keeled over with laughter again.

The other boys came into view at the edge of the ditch and stood there looking down. Michael had never felt so relieved.

Nehor lit another match. "Do you guys like Christmas lights?" He tossed the match.

Michael screamed as his world turned to pain.

McKay State Hospital, San Diego, California. Present Day.

Dr. Nathan Reynolds sipped his water. He sat at a long table with two other forensic psychiatrists and a social worker. The small room was sterile, almost like a morgue, with the permanent scent of Lysol. He took two aspirin from a small bottle in his pocket and washed them down with more water.

"Denied," he said.

The other three on the commitment review board agreed. The file was stamped and passed to an orderly, who stacked it on a table with the rest. The files would later go to the hospital administrator to be entered into the computer. Then the task of letting the patients and their families know whether they could leave or not would be delegated to the staff by the head nurse. In their job, Reynolds knew, shit definitely rolled downhill.

"Who's next?" he asked.

Dr. Cynthia Ami stared at the next file. Reynolds cleared his throat, and she handed it over. He read the name stamped in large red lettering: NEHOR BELL STARK.

"What's his background?" he asked, flipping through the file.

"Anti-social and schizoaffective disorder, we think."

"What do you mean 'we think'? You either know it or you don't."

"He's complex. His MMPI is all over the place. He can take it one day and show extreme anti-social behavior and psychopathy, and the next day, he takes it again, and the results come back within normal range."

"Hm," Reynolds said, impressed. "Rare to learn the test that well. What's his IQ?"

"One seventy-one."

"That can't be right."

"He's been tested multiple times. That's the mean."

"What's this note about pyromania?"

"We thought he had pyromania ideations when he first came in, but since then we haven't seen anything. Most pyromaniacs make drawings or some sort of representations of fires when they can't get the actual thing. He hasn't done that at all. In fact, we conducted a test and left an empty lighter out, pretending that one of the orderlies forgot it, to see what he would do. He picked it up and turned it in to the nurse."

Reynolds studied the file then said, "I don't see any violence or citations."

"No, he's actually quite calm. He hasn't had a single incident while he's been here. There was one thing…" She opened the duplicate file and flipped through some pages. "Ah… yeah, nine years ago. A boy cornered him in the hall and started punching him. But Nehor didn't do anything in response. He didn't even raise his hands to defend himself."

"He just stood there?"

"Until the orderlies arrived, yeah." She cleared her throat. "To be honest, he's quite a charming young man. He's very helpful in the kitchen. He always has any assignments that are due finished early. I don't see a need to keep him here. In therapy, he's shown remarkable insight into his behaviors. I think he's ready to go home and transfer to outpatient."

Reynolds read through the rest of the file. "What kind of name is Nehor anyway?"

"I haven't looked up the etymology, but he comes from an

interesting background. His father was the leader of a small cult in Nevada. His mother escaped with him when he was young and brought him out to California. He doesn't remember his father at all. But Nate, I think he's ready to go. We can give that bed to someone who really needs it."

"Well, he came in when he was twelve, and he's twenty-three now. Unless somebody has a reason we should keep him, I'm inclined to let him go."

Nobody said anything.

Reynolds said, "Released," for the record. He stamped the file and passed it to the orderly. "Who's next?"

CHAPTER 2

Detective Jonathan Stanton looked through the small, dirty window from the attic of the old house. He could see into the bay windows of the house next door. He took a deep breath and checked his watch—past midnight.

The door swung open, and his partner, Stephen Gunn, came in with a pizza and two beers. He put them down on the small table in front of the old futon and opened the beers.

"Beer?" he said.

"No thanks."

"Not thirsty?"

"I don't drink, Stephen. But thanks."

"No shit? Recoverin' alchie?"

"Something like that." Stanton sat down. The television they'd brought up was playing a *Honeymooners* episode. He took a slice of pizza, folded it in half, and took a bite.

"So," Gunn said, "I'm not complainin' or anythin', but do you have any idea why they paired us up?"

"No. I came in last week, and the board was changed. Your name was next to mine. I usually work alone, so I asked Danny about it. He said they wanted all homicide detectives in new pairs now. Policy implemented by the chief."

"Hm. Probably because of that bullshit with Weeks. You hear about that?"

"No."

"Weeks was bangin' an informant for the Salano crew. Turns out the informant was gettin' intel from him and feedin' it back to the crew."

"You're kidding."

"Nope," Gunn said, shaking his head. "You seen Weeks around lately?"

"No."

"'Cause he got knocked down to writin' parkin' tickets."

"Poor guy. I always liked him. Struck me as a little lonely, though."

"Who isn't lonely?"

The noise of an engine interrupted them. Stanton scrambled to his feet and hurried to the window.

A red Ford stopped in the driveway. Two Hispanic men got out and knocked at the side door of the house. A female in a black tube top answered and let them in.

"Looks like Maria has company," Stanton said.

"Who?"

"Not sure. Two Gs. They had tats on the backs of their necks."

"Spiderwebs?"

"Think so. Hard to tell from here."

"That's the Aztec Kings. Street gang in West Hollywood."

"What're gangsters from West Hol doing in San Diego?"

"Nothing good."

Stanton exhaled. "We've been up here three days. This is a waste of time."

"Body's supposed to be cut up at this house, man. That's the word."

"From your snitch who has twenty drug cases against her?"

"From my snitch who'll do anythin' for me to keep her ass outta the can." Gunn slapped his knee. "Sit tight, man. It'll happen." He guzzled half his beer, let out a loud belch, and then leaned back on the futon. "You haven't done too many stakeouts, have you?"

"No."

"That's 'cause you came from Sex Crimes. I got to Homicide through Narcs. That's all I fuckin' *did* was stakeouts. I was up in this shitty bar once in El Cajon for three weeks. I'd come in at nine in the mornin' when they opened and leave at two in the mornin' when they closed. One of the worst times of my life. Got some pussy, though. Those biker chicks are crazy."

Stanton sat back down and put his feet up on the table. "I've seen this episode," he said.

Stanton was awakened by a car door slamming. He looked around. He'd fallen asleep on the futon. Gunn lay on the floor, a pillow under his head and a quilt over him though it was easily eighty degrees.

Stanton went to the window, rubbing sleep out of his eyes. A Chrysler had pulled in next to the Ford, and he reached for the digital recorder on the window that they used to record any notable activity. A skinny Hispanic male stepped out, ran to the door, and pounded on it with his fist. He looked around nervously, and when his eyes flicked across the attic window, Stanton stepped to the side.

When he looked back, the two males they'd seen earlier came out of the house. The three of them ran down to the Chrysler, opened the trunk, and started struggling with a large heavy object covered in black plastic.

"Gunn."

"What?"

"Get up here."

Gunn rolled over and got up. Stanton pointed, and Gunn looked out of the window for a bit before saying, "Holy shit. This is it."

"We gotta get 'em in the house. If we go down while they're outside, they'll run."

"I'll call for backup."

As Gunn put in a call for additional units, Stanton took his Desert Eagle off the nightstand and put on the holster. He caught a glimpse of himself in the mirror over the futon, seeing the deep scarring on his neck from second-degree burns. He pulled his collar up and headed out the door.

Down by the front door, he waited until Gunn came down. All the lights in the house were off, and Stanton had to feel around for the doorknob. When he found it, they slipped out into the warm night.

The neighbor's driveway was gravel, so they moved slowly. Coming around the Chrysler, they looked inside. A white crucifix hung from the rearview mirror.

Stanton looked in the side door of the house. The backup units would take at least fifteen minutes to arrive. He looked back at Gunn.

As if reading his thoughts, Gunn whispered, "Fuck it. Let's go in."

Stanton tried the door. It was locked. Gunn climbed through the window beside it and landed like a cat. He unlocked the door for Stanton.

The kitchen smelled of meat and tomatoes that had been burnt. Stanton quietly shut the door behind him, and they stood, listening to the sounds of the house. Gunn shrugged, and they moved on to the hallway.

The television in the living room was tuned to an all-Spanish channel. The man who'd driven up in the Chrysler was already asleep on the couch. Gunn stepped into a bathroom off the hallway and came out with a hand towel. He stopped behind the man and motioned for Stanton to stand in front of him.

Moving too fast for Stanton to see in the dimly lit room, Gunn wrapped the towel around the man's mouth and shoved it as far in as it would go. He turned him face down on the couch and shoved his face into the cushions, choking off his air. His screams were a muffled whisper.

Stanton yanked the man's arms back and double-locked the cuffs on his wrists. He searched him as the man struggled. No weapon. Gunn pulled his weapon and placed it against the man's head.

"Shh," he whispered, "I don't want this gun to go off accidentally. Do you?" The man quieted down. "Where are your homies?"

The man tried to speak, and Gunn said, "No, no, just nod your head. Are they upstairs?"

He nodded.

"Are they armed?"

He nodded again.

"How many? Nod for each one."

He nodded three times.

"Three with the girl?"

He nodded again.

Stanton said, "We'll wait for the units."

Gunn made a face as if he'd eaten something sour. "They're right upstairs, man. Let's catch these assholes in the act."

"I think we should wait."

The man on the couch started trying to shout again, wiggling to get free. Gunn slapped him on the back of the head and said, "Quiet."

"He could be lying. There could be more of them up there."

"We didn't log anybody but these three and the girl. What, they sneak in through the sewer?" He looked down at the man. "Keep quiet. If you make noise, I'm going to come back downstairs and shoot you up the ass. It takes twenty minutes to die from a shot in the ass. Do you understand?"

Sweat now pouring down his face, he nodded.

"Good." Gunn looked at Stanton. "Come on, partner. Unless you wanna stay downstairs and swap tampons with our girlfriend here." Gunn made for the stairs.

Stanton had an uneasy feeling, but he couldn't let Gunn go up there by himself. He took out a pair of plastic cuffs and snapped them around the man's ankles before following his partner.

The carpeted stairs didn't creak. Gunn went up one side, his back pressed against the wall, and Stanton covered the other side. When they reached the top of the stairs, one of the doors in the hallway was halfway open, and Stanton could see a linoleum floor. He nudged the door open and looked inside.

The nude body of Juan Estrada lay in the bathtub. He'd been a low-level pot and heroin dealer working as a confidential informant for the San Diego PD until he disappeared a week ago. Deep purple bruising on his face and body suggested hours of beatings. His genitals had been cut off, and dozens of cigarette burns covered him.

"Poor bastard," Gunn said, looking over Stanton's shoulder.

A rustling noise came from one of the other rooms—sheets being moved. The detectives looked at each other. Gunn hopped into the shower and hid behind the curtain. Stanton slipped back down the staircase a few steps and lay on his stomach.

A man in boxer shorts and an undershirt came out of one of the rooms and entered the bathroom. He lifted the toilet lid and began to piss. Gunn slowly moved the shower curtain. He caught Stanton's eye and winked.

Gunn leapt from the shower and wrapped his arm around the man's neck, knocking him to the floor with such force that it rattled the house. Gunn kept his hold, landing on top of him and immobilizing him. Stanton ran up the stairs when he heard a female voice coming out of one of the rooms saying, "Jesus, *¿qué está pasando?*"

She looked out of the room and saw Jesus down on the floor of the bathroom with Gunn on top of him. She screamed. Stanton went to quiet her, but the sound of shuffling footsteps coming from another room made him hit the floor. The pop of a handgun echoed through the house, rounds coming through the door on the far side of the hall. The woman took a bullet in the side, and she dropped. Stanton fired through the door five times before the return fire stopped.

Stanton ran to the woman. Blood was pouring out of her and soaking the carpet. He took off his shirt, wadded it up, and pressed it against her wound as he thumbed his radio mic with his other hand. "This is Detective Jonathan Stanton, SDPD, 17469. I need an ambulance at 1327 Rondido Drive. We have a suspect down with a gunshot wound to the abdomen."

Gunn handcuffed Jesus then joined Stanton in the hallway. Gunn flattened himself against the wall and edged over to the door where the shots had come from. Reaching over with one hand, he swung the door open. Inside, Stanton could see a man in boxer shorts with his shirt off, sitting against the bed and facing the door. Blood ran from a bullet hole just above the ear and darkened the sheets behind him. His vacant eyes stared blankly ahead, and a revolver lay in his limp right hand.

Nausea washed over Stanton, even though he had seen far worse. *It must be the physical exertion.* The woman had begun crying, but when he went to comfort her, suddenly he couldn't breathe.

He checked himself for gunshot wounds but found none. Despite that, his lungs squeezed, restricting his airflow as if he were breathing through a straw. Gunn heard him gasping for air and asked, "Hey, man, you okay?"

Before Stanton could respond, his chest tightened like a fist, and pain shocked his body like an electric current. His vision blurred at the edges, and panicking, he hit the floor and lost consciousness.

CHAPTER 3

Nehor Stark stepped out of the McKay State Hospital in San Diego and stood in the parking lot. He looked up at the sun and then shielded his eyes. The hospital had allowed time outside in the yard, but it had still minimized his exposure to sunlight. He was surprised how painful sunlight could be when he hadn't seen it for so long.

He scanned the parking lot. No car, no waiting family, no children or friends or lovers. Only him, the clothes that he wore, and the two hundred dollars he had in his pocket.

The hospital had called a cab for him, and he waited. He'd watched lots of television while inside, but actually seeing the newer models of cars, particularly the shining sports cars that whizzed past, filled him with a sense of wonder, and he smiled. He might have stepped out of a time machine into the future. There were so many things to experience and enjoy, so much fun to be had.

The cab stopped in front of him, and he climbed in. He took a scrap of toilet paper out of his pocket. An address was scribbled on it.

He handed it to the cabbie and turned to stare out the window.

"Who you got up there?" the cabbie said.

Nehor looked at him. "What?" The metallic sound of his voice surprised him. During the past years, he hadn't used it much. In therapy he'd sat quietly and stared at the floor. The doctors assumed his medication had made him inert and let him be.

"At the cemetery. Who you got up there?"

Nehor bit the inside of his cheeks, a habit he had developed out of boredom. "Your wife."

"What?"

He chuckled. "Just drive."

The cabbie mumbled something about assholes in his cab. Nehor watched him. The cabbie clenched his jaw, breathing heavily and occasionally sending a dark look back at Nehor, becoming visibly more upset as he sat and stewed. Finally he pulled to the curb and said, "You know what, asshole? Get out."

"Why?"

"Fuck you, that's why. I don't have to drive nobody I don't want ta. Get out."

Nehor thought about how to respond. *What would somebody say in this situation?* "I'm sorry."

"You're sorry?"

"Yes. I'm sorry. Please, just drive."

"Nah, fuck you, pal. You made your bed. Out."

Nehor took a deep breath and got out of the cab. He'd taken a large serrated knife out of the cafeteria nearly six years ago, and he'd hidden it under his pillow and inside his sleeve when he'd left. He slammed it into one of the tires, nearly up to the hilt. As he pulled it out, air exploded out of the slit, and the cab tilted to the side.

"Motherfucking cocksucker!" the cabbie screamed, jumping out of the cab.

Nehor walked away. The cabbie's hand on his shoulder stopped him. In one clean motion, he spun around with the knife, slicing off all four fingers at the knuckle. The cabbie stood in stunned silence. Nehor glanced down at the severed flesh on the pavement.

"You better pick them up before a cat takes them." He leaned in close to the man's face and whispered, "Here, kitty kitty." He kissed him on the cheek and walked away.

The cabbie stood in shock, but it didn't last. He started yelling and then screaming. Nehor turned around and saw him on his knees picking up his fingers. He smiled and kept walking.

Nehor entered Mount Nadia Memorial Park through the main gates. From its hill, the cemetery had a view of San Diego below it. Residential property surrounded it, but there were few houses, probably because cemeteries routinely brought odd night visitors performing rituals or junkies looking for a quiet place to shoot up.

He stopped at a grave that had a fresh bouquet of flowers on it and picked them up. Many of the graves were simple headstones without décor, and he stepped over them. He had read somewhere that if someone stepped over a grave, the inhabitant could see it and would want revenge.

The sunlight faded as gray clouds wafted in, and a slight drizzle began. The warm rain trickled down through his hair, which he decided he wanted to shave, and over his face. It soaked his clothes and the flowers in his hand.

By the time he found the grave he was drenched from head to foot. He sat down cross-legged on the wet grass and placed the flowers on the grave. It was a modest headstone, dark gray with two simple lines: ESTELL ROSE STARK - BELOVED MOTHER.

Nehor breathed deeply through his nose and pulled the hair out of his eyes, slicking it back on his head. He ran his hand along the headstone and the engraved lettering.

In a sudden, violent motion he bashed the headstone with his foot again and again and again. He took the flowers and whipped them against the headstone until they disintegrated, and then he dug into the grass with his bare fingers. He dug with both hands, grunting and spitting and swearing, until he had thoroughly exhausted himself.

Warm sweat mixed with the rain on his forehead as he fell back, out of breath. Despite his effort, the hole was only half a foot deep. He lay looking up at the sky for a long time, feeling the rain on his face, catching his breath. He stood up and saw a small shack on the property. He walked down to it and found the door unlocked. The small toolshed held a lot of tools, a wheelbarrow, a desk with several documents on it, and a mug of coffee. He tasted the coffee. It was cold, and he spit it out, splattering the wall.

He took a shovel, headed back to the grave, and dug around it until the headstone was unstable and he could kick it over. The stone weighed more than the size had led him to expect. He managed to get it over to the pavement of the road up the hill, where he lifted it over his head and threw it down. It broke into three pieces. He threw the pieces several times, but they wouldn't break into smaller chunks.

Nehor stood there, staring at the bits of headstone. The silent homes around him reminded him he didn't have a place to stay.

As he descended the hill, physically exhausted but with his mind fizzing with wiry energy that provided a second wind, he could see the outline of the city. He grinned, imagining how much fun he was about to have.

CHAPTER 4

Stanton waited patiently at Scripps Hospital for the results of his neurological testing. Diagrams and charts of the brain's anatomy covered the walls, along with a poster from the '80s. It showed an egg frying and said, *This is your brain on drugs.*

A nurse came in and took his medical charts. Stanton could see the markings on her forearm of a tattoo that had been removed: a man's name with a heart underneath.

"The doctor will be right with you."

Stanton took a deep breath and leaned back in the chair. He had suffered a deep depression as a child. His parents had taken him to a child psychiatrist. His father, a successful psychiatrist himself, had felt helpless before his son's malaise.

The psychiatrist had been quirky and fun but unable to help him. Stanton stopped going. When they moved from rain-soaked Seattle to San Diego, with its 320 days of sunshine and the beach, Stanton pulled out of the depression. Being back in a hospital having doctors trying to figure out what was wrong with him made him feel like that kid again, sitting in front of a psychiatrist who knew there was nothing he could do for him.

A knock interrupted his thoughts, and Dr. Kumar Patel stepped in. A gold bracelet flashed against his dark skin. He sat down next to Stanton before he looked up from the charts.

"Well, we weren't able to find anything, Jon. Motor activity is fine; there are no meningeal symptoms. Cranial nerves, sensory system, and coordination… everything is fine. The MRI didn't show any abnormal lesions or subarachnoid or intracranial hemorrhages. Physically, there's nothing wrong with you."

"That's kind of what I figured. I thought it might've been fatigue."

"That's possible, but I don't think that's what it was. I think you had a panic attack."

"Now? I'm thirty-six. Why would they begin now?"

"It's rare. Usually they show up sooner, but you know as well as I do that they can happen later in life. You have a PhD in psychology— think about it clinically. If a patient came to you with a job as stressful as yours, divorced, working long hours, and he described this incident, what would be your first thoughts for a diagnosis?"

Stanton exhaled through his nose and focused on a poster on the wall. "Stress-induced panic disorder."

"I'm referring you to a specialist. She's a psychiatrist I went to medical school with." The doctor rose. "I still remember the class you taught at UCLA on cognition and schizophrenia. You were one of the best professors I had. I was a little jealous 'cause you were younger than me. If you don't mind my asking, why didn't you go to medical school or stick with the University? What made you want to be a cop?"

"Right now, Kumar, I have no idea."

Stanton sat in his car, enjoying the heater as it rained outside. He turned on some music and closed his eyes. He felt fine and comfortable. But when he began thinking about work, about the stacks of files on his desk, the tight feeling in his chest returned. Each file was a life—a life somebody else destroyed. And like a stone thrown into a pond, the ripples affected everything. Families were devastated; friends were left in shock; and teachers, church leaders, and neighbors would begin being a little more cautious. Perhaps they wouldn't get so attached to people in the future, at least subconsciously, for fear of something like this happening again.

Stanton felt lightheaded. He took out his phone to look at the contact he had just added for Dr. Jennifer S. Palmer and dialed. A receptionist answered. He explained that he was a referral from Dr. Patel and that they would be faxing over paperwork later in the day. An appointment was set for tomorrow morning, and he hung up.

As he started his car and pulled out, he felt jittery. In the macho, testosterone-driven world of homicide detectives, therapy was seen as a weakness. Many—if not most—of the detectives were in therapy, on medication, or in need of one or the other. But it was never spoken about.

Stanton's cell phone rang—Lieutenant Childs.

"What's up, Danny?"

"Hey. How was the visit to the hospital?"

"Fine."

"That's it? Just fine?"

"They didn't find anything wrong."

"I figured that. It's nerves, man. It happens. Pressure builds up in the job, and it needs a release. If you don't give it one, it'll take one itself. That's why I keep tellin' you to come boxin' with me."

"I don't think getting punched in the face is going to help me very much. But thanks."

"Suit yourself. Anyway, what the hell was I sayin'? Oh, yeah. I got a case for you and Gunn. Body found in a burned-down house. Could be electrical wires or suicide, or shit knows what. Dude was an old man and probably lit himself on fire fallin' asleep with a cigarette in his mouth. There was a sixteen-year-old stepson who lived with him. You want me to upload the file onto the server?"

"No, I'll take a hard copy."

"New world, brother. You gotta stay up on technology."

"I like having a file. There's something comforting about it. It's real, not just information on a network."

"Well, get your no-computer-havin' ass back here then and pick up the file. I got the fire investigator meetin' you down there in two hours."

"Thanks. I'll swing by after lunch."

Stanton hung up. Fires were usually the most boring of all his cases but the easiest to close. Nine times out of ten, they were as Childs described them: somebody left a cigarette out near a quilt or didn't wire something properly or left flammable material near a furnace.

As he stopped for lunch, he glanced down at his phone and

Googled: *stress induced panic disorder treatments.*

CHAPTER 5

Stanton sat outside the burnt-out shell of a house and sipped a Diet Coke. The neighborhood was quiet and upper-middle class, the type of place where something like this would be talked about and dissected for years to come.

The home was a two-story brick-and-stucco with a small front lawn. Police tape hung across the windows, which had been blown out during the fire. The exterior was charred around the windows and front door.

A car came to a stop in front of him. Gunn saluted him with two fingers. Stanton nodded and took out his phone and texted him.

Where's the fire investigator?

sleepin' with yo mama

my mother's dead, jerk

really? what kind of sick fuck do we have as a fire investigator?

Stanton grinned. An old Ford truck pulled up in front of the house. A man got out wearing a bomber jacket and took a kit from the bed of the truck. Stanton approached him.

"Are you Benny?"

"Yeah. You Jon Stanton?"

"Yeah," Stanton said, shaking his hand.

"Looks like we got ourselves a little barbeque."

"A man was killed in that house," Stanton said.

"Don't mind him," Gunn said, walking up. "His mother died recently."

"Really? I'm sorry to hear that."

"She didn't die recently. Can we get on with this?"

Benny shrugged and looked the house over. He took glasses out of his breast pocket and slipped them on. "Let's get this party off the ground."

They walked up the lawn to the front door. Then Benny walked back down to the lawn and all the way around the house, taking pictures. Stanton and Gunn quietly followed behind. He took ten photos of the exterior then pulled out a pen and graph paper and began making diagrams. Gunn sat down on the porch, surfing the internet while they waited.

"Okay," Benny finally said, "let's go inside."

The interior smelled like a campfire and melted tires. Benny glanced around and turned down the hall to the bedroom. He looked at the kitchen, another bedroom, and then the living room, and then he stopped and took the camera out again.

"You start where there's the least damage," he said. "That means the fire didn't start there. See? There's just smoke and heat damage here. Now we follow that back to the source."

In the hallway, wires hung from the destroyed ceiling, and some sort of sticky ash on the ground clung to Stanton's shoes. They were his nice shoes, and he wished he'd kept some sneakers in his car.

Benny removed some debris at the end of the hallway, and the three men noticed charring at the base of the wall. "See here?" Benny said, pointing. "Gases become buoyant when they burn, so they rise, and that means the flame does, too. These char marks that look like puddles, they show the flames were burning low, there. But now, we follow the burn trail down the hallway."

Gunn leaned close to Stanton from behind him and whispered, "Since when is he a fuckin' professor?"

The bedroom on the far right, where the responding officers had found the body, had been cleared out. Sunlight came in through the broken windows.

"We got pour patterns here. See, if the fire's burning low, it means a liquid accelerant was used. And look at that glass there, those broken pieces by the window. See those spider web-patterned cracks? That's called crazed glass. The fire has to burn hot to make the glass do that, which means an accelerant was used. What you got here is someone who poured something over this house and lit it on fire. You got yourselves a murder."

"What are these Vs?" Gunn said.

"The smoke and heat from fire goes outward, so when something catches fire, the scorching and charring creates that V pattern. The bottom of the V points to a place of origin for that particular flame. I noticed one out there in the hallway, too. That means you got one point of origin in here and one out there. One accidental fire, maybe, but not two at the same time. This was started by someone."

Gunn nodded. "Son of a bitch, you are the professor."

"Doesn't make sense," Stanton said. "If they would've poured an accelerant over the entryway and by the windows, the vic couldn't have gotten past them to get out. If someone wanted to kill him, why didn't they create a fire wall and lock him in? Why would they pour it in such random places?"

Benny spit near the wall. "Who the hell knows? That's you guys' department. I told you this here was a murder, and I bet if you talk to that stepson o' his, you'll find out he was the one that did it."

Stanton opened the file in his hand. The victim's name was Marco Yazzie. The stepson was Fernando Yazzie. Fernando had been home when the fire began. He ran out of the house screaming, calling for help. Several neighbors ran over. In their initial statements they'd said he was frantic.

"Well, should we go have a chat with the Son of the Year?" Gunn said.

"Looks like it."

"You wanna grab something to eat first?"

"I'm not hungry. I'll just meet you down at the precinct. Is he already in custody?"

"Yup. They picked him up a few hours ago from school."

They left the house. Stanton saw Benny making notes on a clipboard. He waved goodbye as he walked to his truck.

Back at the precinct, Stanton went straight to his office and shut the door. He reviewed the Yazzie file again, reading the initial responding detective's report. The victim had died of smoke inhalation before he was engulfed by the fire. Stanton glanced at the photos and shuffled them to the back of the file.

He stretched his neck and closed the file before turning to his computer. Opening his email, he saw he had eighty-seven unread messages.

Nearly an hour later, Gunn showed up at the precinct. He walked through quietly, nodding to a few people before coming into Stanton's office without knocking. He sat down across from him and put his feet up on the desk. Ten minutes passed before Stanton spoke.

"You smell like booze."

"Haven't touched the stuff today. Well, ten shots. Give or take."

"You can't come in drunk on every case. Eventually someone will notice."

"Someone will notice because I ain't actin' right, or someone will notice because someone else will tell them?"

"I'm not like that, Stephen."

"No? You sure as hell testified against Harlow pretty quick."

Stanton stopped typing and turned to him. "What did you say?"

"I'm just sayin', you tell me you're not a rat, and I tell you that you're the only detective here that's testified against another cop."

He turned back to the computer. "Michael Harlow wasn't a cop. He was a thug. I took another thug off the street when I testified against him. That's all we do. That's our job."

"This ethics lecture is borin' me," he said, leaning farther back in the chair. "Let's go get some pussy."

"Not interested."

"Man, twenty homicide detectives and I get stuck with the Mormon."

"It's not exactly charming from where I'm sitting either."

Silence stretched between them. "I didn't mean that," Gunn said. "I really didn't. You're dependable, and there's no one else I'd want watchin' my back. But you gotta cut loose sometimes, man. At least a little. I feel like I'm hangin' out with my grandma sometimes."

Stanton finished the email he was working on and sent it. He stood up and turned to Gunn. "I'll try to be more fun if you quit showing up to work drunk."

"I'll try."

They left the office and headed down the long corridor. To the right were the holding cells, to the left the front commons area and the entrance, where two officers were tackling a man who was resisting. One of the officers tased him. He was screaming, and they had to hurry and get the cuffs on him before he regained his composure. Stanton had to step over the pool of urine that was running down the man's leg and onto the floor.

CHAPTER 6

Stanton brought a cold soda into the hot interrogation room with no windows and set it on the table in front of sixteen-year-old Fernando. He sat across from him and smiled as he opened a bottle of juice for himself. Fernando watched him for a moment and then opened the soda and took a swig.

"I saw in your file from school that you play baseball. What position?"

"Shortstop."

"I played catcher, but I was too skinny so they sent me to left field. I remember there wasn't much to do there, but I would get a chance to just hang out in the sunshine and think about things. It was much more enjoyable than being catcher."

"How long did you play for?"

"Just one season. I never really got into sports until I took up surfing."

Gunn walked in then, his hair wet and slicked back and his face freshly washed. Stanton knew he had been in the bathroom splashing cold water on himself.

Fernando looked at Gunn and then back to Stanton and said, "I've been playing since I was six. I was gonna go to college on a scholarship. That was my plan."

"Why do you say it 'was' your plan?"

"I don't know. I ain't got no other family. I might be put in a foster home. I've heard bad stories about people my age that get put into foster homes, and I don't know if they're gonna let me play baseball."

Stanton leaned a little closer to the table. "I'm sorry about what happened to your stepfather, Fernando."

"He was a good guy. He took me in when my mom died, and he took care of me. He was the one who got me into baseball. He said that was my way out."

"Out of what?"

"The life, man. I got two older brothers, and they're both in prison. Where I come from, you play sports, or you stand on the corner and sell dope. There's no other way out."

"He sounds like he was a good father."

Gunn was leaning against the wall and looking at his shoes. "My old man bought me a hooker when I was fourteen. He said I was a man and that's what men do. That's the only thing the son of a bitch ever bought me."

Stanton looked at him then back to Fernando. "Can you tell me what you remember about the fire?"

"I was asleep in my room. I was just there on the bed, and I heard my pops yelling for me."

"What happened then?"

"I got up, and there was smoke everywhere. It was coming in through my door, and I started coughing and stuff. I ran out into the hall 'cause he was yelling for me, but I felt like I was gonna pass out. There was fire everywhere. It was all in the hallway, and I couldn't get to him." Tears welled up in his eyes. "I couldn't get to him."

"Fernando, listen to me. You did everything you could. No one expected you to be able to save him. It was out of your hands."

Gunn said, "Did you see how the fire started?"

"No."

"So you just woke up and the house was on fire, huh? That seems weird that you didn't smell nothin'."

Fernando shrugged and looked down to the table. He began to play with the soda can. Stanton could tell he was shutting down.

"Stephen, would you mind if Fernando and I just talked for a minute?"

Gunn looked at him, frowning. "Yeah, sure."

When the door closed behind Gunn, Stanton took a sip of his juice and leaned back in the chair. "His family's not close. He doesn't know what it's like to lose somebody."

"Do you?"

"Yeah, my mother. She died of breast cancer when I was a lot younger. I was with her through those times. The hospital cafeteria cook had my dinner ready for me every night 'cause I was there so much."

Tears came to Fernando's eyes again, and he wiped them with the back of his hand. Stanton gently placed his hand on his wrist. They sat quietly for a long time as Fernando wept softly.

When he was through, Stanton stood up. "I'll be right back."

He stepped out of the room and saw Gunn staring through the two-way mirror. He didn't acknowledge Stanton as he walked by.

Stanton went back to his office and flipped through the contacts on his phone. He found the number he was looking for and dialed. A female voice answered.

"Hello?"

"Hi, Cami. It's Jon."

"Hey! How are you? I haven't talked to you in a minute."

"I know. Sorry about that. I've been swamped up here. How's Hank doing?"

"Great. He's been focusing more on commercial real estate and leaving the residential stuff for the young kids. He works fewer hours and likes his clientele more."

"That's good news. Please tell him hi for me and that we'll go golfing again soon."

"I will. So what can I do for you?"

"I was wondering if you could pull some strings and have a kid placed with a family."

"For you, anything. Tell me about him."

"He's sixteen, and his mother died some time ago. His stepfather took care of him since then, and he just passed away in a fire. I think he needs a family that doesn't have anybody else his same age. He seems shy and introverted. He'd do really well with a couple or with a couple who have young children."

"Okay. I'm not at the office now, but when I head back I'll find someplace good. Can you email me his info?"

"Sure thing. I'm going to keep him here at the station for now. How quickly can we do it?"

"We could get him in tomorrow or the next day if I rush. You can place him in a group home for now."

"No, I'll put him up in a hotel. Can you let me know as soon as you have a place lined up?"

"You got it."

"Thanks, Cami. Take care."

"You too. Bye."

Stanton went back out to the front desk. He checked the roster and saw that a young rookie named McManis was on duty at the front desk. He hunted him down, finding him in the break room eating some Twinkies.

"Got a kid here who we're putting up in a hotel. There's a Marriott a couple of miles west near Greenview. I need you to take him there." Stanton took out his credit card and handed it to him. "Use this to pay. And tell the front desk to allow him any meals he wants."

McManis rolled his eyes but took the credit card.

Stanton went back to the observation room.

Gunn was still standing there, his arms folded. "So we gonna actually drill this little shit or what?"

"No."

"And, oh, great and wise Jonathan, may I ask why not?"

Stanton ignored the sarcasm. "He didn't do it."

"What? You think you can tell that from a two-minute conversation about baseball?"

"I'm telling you, Stephen, he didn't do it. I'm putting him up in a hotel for tonight, and tomorrow he's gonna be placed in a good foster home. He's got no relatives to go to."

"Hey, fuck that. He's our prime—no, our *only* suspect in a homicide, and you're just gonna let him go?"

"I don't think it was a homicide."

"You heard the arson investigator just like I did."

"He came to his decision too quickly. He was just processing the scene to match a hunch he had. It wasn't objective; he wasn't listening to the evidence."

Gunn shook his head. "You don't know shit about arson

investigations, Jon. And neither do I. Let's leave it to the experts."

"I intend to."

CHAPTER 7

Monique Gaspirini locked up the H&M store at ten, leaned against the glass, and sighed. It had been a long day. Two girls had cancelled on her, and she had to open and close. And on top of that, the rush hadn't even given her time to grab lunch. The mall had been so packed that at one point, they'd run out of bags and customers had to carry their items out.

"Hey," Dylan said as he walked up, "those guys left their number for you."

"Which guys?"

"Those forty-year-old douchebags with the shiny hair. I think they were Iranian or something."

"Oh, great. You can just toss it."

"You're on a roll, Mon. At least half the guys that came in today wanted to fuck you."

She patted his cheek. "If you weren't gay, you could totally have me."

"Interesting offer, sweetheart, but you couldn't handle this."

He did the silliest sexy dance that she had ever seen. She burst out laughing and slapped his shoulder.

He said, "Jasper and Matt are still here. We'll finish up. You go home."

"You sure?"

"Yeah, you worked since opening. Go home and get some sleep."

She kissed his cheek then went in back and got her purse and cell phone and headed out the door, waving to Jasper and Matt, who were goofing around on the escalator. Monique headed out of the mall, stopping briefly at a kiosk to buy some licorice, and had to ring the alarm on her car to find it—parked several dozen meters away in employee parking. She groaned at the thought of walking any farther in her high heels.

The Toyota Prius looked worn out, and she wondered if it was the best idea to keep taking it up in the canyons. Her younger brother had even tried four-wheeling with it once, and it had gotten stuck within a matter of minutes.

There were footsteps behind her as she opened the door and she glanced back.

A couple was making out by their Tahoe. She had her hand down his pants, and he was grunting like a pig.

"Ew, gross. There are kids running around here." She got into her car.

The air was cool, and no clouds darkened the night. The sky sparkled with stars, and she glanced at it whenever there was a pause in the bumper-to-bumper traffic on the freeway.

She eventually got off at exit 197 and passed Alejandro's, a restaurant owned by the father of a friend of hers.

She lived alone in a house on Maplewood Drive. Her parents were the only people who occasionally stayed with her, but they preferred to travel. The Old West-style house had six bedrooms on three levels, all packed with furniture her parents had decided not to throw out, even if the pieces had passed their prime. Having the same furniture she'd had when she was growing up was comforting, and she just didn't have the heart to get rid of any of it.

Inside, the ceilings were high and the space open, with fine oriental rugs over the old carpet. Monique tossed her purse on the coffee table and collapsed on the couch, holding her arm over her forehead for a few minutes. She then took a deep breath and rose to go into the kitchen.

She didn't really see anything in the fridge that she felt like eating. She took out a beer and had a long drink from the bottle before pouring the rest into a glass. She was about to return to the living room when she noticed the door.

The back door of the house had two locks and a doggie door, though she had gotten rid of the dog long ago. And the door was ajar.

She put her beer down and went over. It was definitely open and more than a couple of inches. She thought back over the day. Had she used this door at all? She might have left it open last night, as she'd gone on a date and gotten drunk at dinner. But would she have forgotten it today when she left for work?

Monique shut the door and locked it. She glanced out the window at the backyard and saw nothing but grass.

As she made her way to the front hallway and the staircase leading to the second level, she decided she would have to be more careful. Though she lived in a safe neighborhood, a few of her neighbors had reported thefts.

She undressed in her bedroom, then went into the bathroom and hopped in the shower. The water took a moment to warm up, and rather than stand outside and wait for it, she stood right under the water and felt the exhilarating cold against her skin. She let it run down her back and over her legs as she lathered her hair.

She soaped herself up with body wash and rinsed. Then she brushed her teeth before stepping out and wrapping herself in a towel. On her way down the hallway to her bedroom she passed a window that overlooked the backyard. There, under the light of the back porch, a man stood staring up at her.

She gasped. His face was pale, and he was bald. He smiled crookedly and waved to her.

She ran to the bedroom and grabbed the phone. As she dialed 911, she went to stand on the top step. There were enough stairs that even if he were to sprint for her, she could make it into the bedroom and lock the door.

Monique could see the kitchen from here. The back door was open again.

"Nine-one-one operator, how may I assist you?"

"This is Monique Gaspirini," she said, panic creeping into her voice, "I live at 1413 Maplewood Drive, and there's a man in my house."

"Where is he now?"

"I think he's inside the house. I shut the back door, and it's open again now."

"Can you get out of the house?"

"No, I'm upstairs. Well, I might be able to climb out the window in my bedroom."

"Does your bedroom door lock?"

"Yes."

"Go in there right now for me, Monique, and lock the door."

She did and leaned against it. "Okay."

"Now I want you to go by the window and plan to climb down, okay? If you hear him come up the stairs you start climbing down, but not before. Is it a long drop?"

"Maybe fifteen feet."

"Okay, well, I'm gonna stay on the phone with you, okay? The police will be there shortly."

"Okay."

"Are you near the window?"

"Yes."

Downstairs, someone shut the back door and walked across the linoleum in the kitchen. Everything was silent for a moment, and she didn't breathe. The dispatcher kept talking, but Monique had lowered the phone, listening intently to what was going on downstairs.

She'd lived in this house for twenty-three years and knew exactly what the quiet, barely audible but unmistakable sound was. Someone was climbing the stairs and had made them creak.

"Oh, fuck me," she said. "He's in the house. He's in the house right now, and he's coming up the stairs!"

"Okay, calm down, just do what I said and climb out the window."

Wrapping the towel tightly around herself, she opened the window as far as it would go and kicked the screen out. It fell, clattering on the driveway. She put one foot out and tried to hold the phone with one hand while she balanced with the other but couldn't do it. She pinned the phone in between her ear and shoulder and used both hands to climb out.

The air was warm, but it still gave her goose bumps as she put her other leg on the ledge just underneath her window. She could hear from inside the house—he was almost to the top of the stairwell.

There was an overhang covering part of the driveway to her right about six feet down. If she could land on it she wouldn't be hurt, but if she missed, she would fall to the ground and hit cement.

From the distance came another sound: sirens.

They were loud, and startling, and annoying… and she had never heard anything more comforting in her life.

The knob on the bedroom door turned one way and then the other, and someone pushed on the door. She screamed. The operator began yelling, asking what was going on, and Monique jumped.

She hit the covering hard and felt her ankle roll. The phone flew out of her hand onto the cement below, shattering. She lay there, crying as she rubbed her ankle, looking up at her bedroom window.

The sirens were on her street and the police had arrived: two cruisers. Two officers got out of the first car. They didn't see her until she shouted for them, and they came over and helped her down.

"He's inside," she said.

They ran into the house. She folded her arms and limped over to one of the police cruisers and leaned against it as the second cruiser with another officer pulled up. A few of her neighbors had come out onto their porches to see what the commotion was about, and she ignored them and kept her eyes glued to the house. One of the officers tried to take down the details. She could see lights going on throughout the house, even her basement. The lights stayed on. After what seemed like an hour but was closer to fifteen minutes, the officers came back outside.

"There's no one in there, ma'am."

"He was in there," she said, pointing. "I saw him. He was in the backyard and he—he waved to me, and then I heard footsteps and—and that's when I called you guys."

"Are you sure it wasn't one of your neighbors?"

"I know what my fucking neighbors look like. There was a stranger in my house."

"Well, we'll do one more walk-through and fill out a report. Didn't look like anything was damaged, and no one was hurt. If you see him again, give us a call."

"That's it? Someone broke into my house, and that's all you're gonna do?"

"I saw the beer out. How much have you had to drink?"

"Part of one bottle. I'm not drunk. I'm telling you someone was in my fucking house."

The other officer finally chimed in. "There's been some reports of thefts around here. We was at your neighbor's house just across the street a couple weeks ago. That might be what it is. Someone's stealing things people leave out, stuff outta the garage, things like that. That's probably all it was."

"He looked crazy. He didn't look normal."

"Since when are criminals normal?"

The other officer said, "We'll take your info. Do you have anywhere to sleep tonight?"

"Yeah, I can go to my boyfriend's house."

"Well, why don't you do that for tonight if you're too scared to stay here? There wasn't any damage to the door, so I'm guessing it was left open."

"No, I locked it. I know I did."

"Make sure to lock all your doors," he said, ignoring her statement.

The other officer looked over the house. "If he was in there, he ain't now. We'll do a quick spin around the neighborhood. Maybe we'll get lucky. We'll forward your case to a detective, and he'll probably call you tomorrow to follow up. Pay a visit to the house, maybe."

They took the rest of her information, walked through the house one more time, and promised that a report would be filed. She watched from the porch as they drove away. Turning to her house, she knew she wouldn't be able to sleep here tonight. She would go to her boyfriend's, and then he would have to sleep over here with her until her parents got home.

Monique went inside to gather her things. She shut and locked the front door and then checked that all the doors and windows throughout the house had been locked, as well. Only then did she remember she was in a towel. She had wondered why one of the officers kept looking at her chest.

She went upstairs to her bedroom and had begun to gather some clothes when she heard a sound coming from downstairs.

As she stood up, listening, out of the corner of her eye she saw the slightest movement inside her closet. Instinctively and without any thought, she ran.

Laughter sounded behind her as arms wrapped around her throat, and she slammed into the floor.

CHAPTER 8

Detective Stephen Gunn climbed the stone steps of the government housing project and stopped at some graffiti on the wall. It was beautifully done: an Aztec or Mayan warrior cutting off the head of an enemy, a nude woman at his feet. It took up most of the wall. Gangs had tagged over it—graffiti had been vandalized.

Savages, he thought, climbing the steps.

On the top floor he knocked at the thick wooden door of apartment 4612 and waited. He heard someone shuffling inside, and the music playing on a stereo was turned down. Someone leaned against the door and stared out of the peephole, and then the lock clicked and the chain rattled.

The woman who opened the door would have been beautiful if not for the premature aging. Wrinkles surrounded her eyes and lips, and her once bright blonde hair looked greasy and dull. But her sapphire eyes were still vibrant, and Gunn admired them before brushing past her and into the apartment.

He glanced at the porn on the television and went to the fridge. He popped the top off a beer before flopping onto the couch and picking up the remote.

"I'm watching that," the woman said, sitting next to him.

"You really a nympho, or is that just an act?"

"We all got our demons."

"This and the heroin you was shootin' up before I got here? Did the guy you were with jump off the balcony?"

"Don't look at me like that, Stephen. I hate that."

"Like what?"

"Like I'm some whore that you can just come over and fuck whenever you want."

He grabbed her by the back of the head and pulled her close to put his lips over hers and run his tongue inside her mouth. "You are." He pinned her arms down on the couch and pushed up her nightgown as he unzipped his pants and entered her. The sex was rough, and she slapped him hard several times. By the end they were both drenched in sweat.

Gunn rolled off her, and they lay on the couch as the porno kept playing. He reached over to the remote and changed it to a baseball game.

"You got anythin' for me?" Gunn said.

"No. Everything's really quiet. No one's making any moves."

"What about our friend Ricardo?"

"No, he's lying low." She sat up, pulling her nightgown over herself. "If I didn't let you fuck me, what would you do?"

"I'd arrest you for the dope you got in here and then call your parole officer and have you sent back to prison."

"Would you really do that? I know you threaten it 'cause you think you need to to get what you want, but would you really do that to me?"

He pushed her out of the way to watch the screen. "Yes."

She stood up quietly and went into the bathroom. The shower ran, and she came out later in jeans and a sweatshirt. She collapsed onto the La-Z-Boy next to the television and began to nod off. Gunn watched her and shook his head.

"That shit's gonna kill you."

"I know."

"Do you wanna die?"

"Yes."

"Jaime, drop the shit. Let's get you cleaned up. Aren't you sick of livin' like this?"

"You're one to judge me," she said, her eyes closing and then darting wide again.

He sat up and guzzled the rest of his beer and then went back to the fridge for another. When he returned, she'd leaned her head back on the chair and closed her eyes. He'd dealt with her enough to know she wouldn't actually be asleep for the next six or seven hours.

"If I asked you to marry me," he said, "would ya?"

"Yes."

"Would you get clean for me?"

"I don't wanna get clean."

"Do you have other guys like me?"

"What d'ya mean?"

"Do you have guys that come over and fuck you and sleep in your bed? Do you cook them breakfast?"

"Yes, I cook them breakfast."

"How many other guys?"

"I don't know."

"Five?"

"Maybe."

"Ten?"

"I don't know, maybe."

He took a swig of beer. "You are a whore. And you're dreamin' if you think I'd marry a whore."

"Why not?" she said, a slight smile on her lips. "Your mother was a whore."

He jumped from the couch and grabbed her by the hair. "Don't you ever talk about my mother."

She laughed.

He kissed her, and she wrapped her arms around him as he lifted her and carried her into the bedroom.

CHAPTER 9

Jon Stanton sat in the waiting room of Dr. Jennifer Palmer and stared at the imitation classical Greek statue near the receptionist's desk. A nude male carved out of marble was standing on a ball, and ants were carrying him somewhere. It looked fairly new. He was stuck in a pose of anguish with his arm above his head, flexing his perfectly carved abdominal muscles.

"Mr. Stanton?"

"Yes," he said, his gaze still on the statue.

"Dr. Palmer is ready to see you now."

"Thank you."

He went through the brushed-wood double doors. A woman in her mid-thirties sat at a large glass desk. Her hair was pulled back, and she wore a skirt and a shell top with heels. She glanced up and smiled.

"Jennifer Palmer, Detective. Nice to meet you." She rose and shook his hand.

"Pleasure."

"Please, have a seat over here if you don't mind."

She led him to two brown leather chairs, and he sat down across from her. One wall of her office was made entirely of glass and looked down over the city. Stanton glanced out at the clouds overhead and then back to Dr. Palmer, who was quietly waiting for him to turn to her.

"I understand from your physician that you've had an episode."

"I suppose so. I don't know if I would call it that. All the neurological tests came back negative, so he thinks it might be psychological."

"Do you think that?"

"I don't know. I don't see why they would hit me now."

"What would hit you now?"

"Panic attacks."

She nodded. "Dr. Patel told me you had a doctorate in psychology and that your father was a psychiatrist. But you chose to abandon the field for police work."

"Yeah."

"What does your father think about that?"

"I don't know. I haven't spoken to him since my mother's death almost… almost twenty years ago."

"Why haven't you spoken to him?"

"We were never that close. He approached everything from an intellectual perspective, and I didn't."

"How did you approach it?"

"I always thought feeling and imagination were more important than knowledge. Or at least *as* important. He didn't see it that way."

"Did he treat you differently because of that?"

"I think so. In the end we both realized we disliked the kind of person the other was."

"How was your relationship with your mother, Jon? You don't mind if I call you Jon, do you?"

"Not at all. It was good. Once the relationship with my father became strained, I started spending less time with her, too. I always regretted that. By the time I realized it, it was too late. She was already diagnosed with stage-four breast cancer."

"I'm sorry to hear that. No matter how old you are, the death of a parent is always traumatic."

"Yeah, it was. She was really the only family I had. I don't know any of my cousins or aunts and uncles. I didn't know my grandparents… When she was gone, that was it."

"Have you tried contacting your father?"

"Once, on the phone. He was really standoffish then said he had to go and hung up. I don't think he's forgiven me for converting to Mormonism."

"Really? What faith is he?"

"He's an atheist, as hardened as you could be. He finds the entire idea of religion—not just the practical application, but the idea itself—ludicrous. To him, anyone that's gullible enough to get suckered into religion doesn't deserve any sympathy. He told me once that religious people shouldn't be allowed to vote."

"Are you a devout Mormon?"

"Yes."

"I can see why there's tension between you and your father. Have you talked to him about your conversion?"

"Just when I invited him to my baptism, when I was eighteen. He refused to come."

She was silent and just nodded. "I'd like to talk about this episode that occurred. Were you thinking about your father at the time?"

"No."

"What were you thinking about?"

"I don't know. Nothing, I guess. We had raided a house, and an innocent girl had gotten shot. The perp was in the bed. He was sitting up with a gunshot wound to the head, and all his blood was emptying onto the bed."

"That's pretty graphic. Were you disturbed by that?"

"No."

"Most people would be. Why were you not, do you think?"

"I don't know. You get used to it. Or at least you convince yourself you do. But when I saw it, I started feeling lightheaded, and then my chest started tightening. Before I knew what was happening, I passed out."

"What did you feel, Jon, the second you saw that body? What was the thought in your head?"

"I thought how hard it was going to be for someone to get that blood stain out of those sheets."

She laughed, and covered her mouth. "I am so sorry. That just wasn't the answer I was expecting." She scribbled down a few notes on a legal pad and cleared her throat. "Is that the first time you've ever had something like that occur? The panic attack, I mean."

"Yes."

"Are you on any medications, Jon?"

"No."

She stood up and took a prescription pad off her desk. "With your permission, I would like to write you a prescription for Xanax."

"I don't have anxiety."

She glanced at him, and her eyes went down his arm to his fingers. He was rubbing his index finger and thumb together and hadn't even noticed he was doing it until her gaze fixed on it. He stopped and put his hand on the armrest.

"There's nothing wrong with medication, Jon. From what Dr. Patel told me about your work, it sounds like these attacks aren't just an annoyance. Your life is at stake because of the situations you're put in. I think the Xanax will calm them, make them more manageable." She handed him the scrip and sat back down across from him. "I'd like to talk a little bit more about your father, if you don't mind."

Stanton glanced out the window. The clouds had accumulated, and he could tell that rain would soon follow. He folded the slip of paper, put it in his jacket pocket, and leaned back in the chair. "I had a sister, too."

CHAPTER 10

Emma Lyon answered her phone on the third ring, and her receptionist said that her two thirty appointment was here.

"Send him in," she said.

She glanced around her office as she waited and decided that she really needed to straighten up. It was typical for a professor's office: shelves upon shelves of endless books, a few diplomas hung on the walls, papers stacked a foot high on her desk. The office was small, and it would've made most people feel claustrophobic, but she found it comforting. Like an old sweater she'd thoroughly broken in. Above her door was a sign that read: Chemists Do It Subatomically.

She watched as the homicide detective walked in and shut the door behind him. He was carrying an iPad under his arm and wore a pinstripe sports coat with jeans and a tie. He had boyish good looks, and despite herself, she knew she was blushing.

"Jon Stanton," he said.

"Emma Lyon," she said, rising and shaking his hand. He stood there a while. "Oh, sorry. Please have a seat."

"So how do you like teaching here?"

"UCLA or Los Angeles?"

"UCLA."

"It's great. I get a lot of support, a lot of time to pursue research interests. Did you go here?"

"No, I taught here for a couple of semesters."

"Really? Criminal justice?"

"No, psychology."

"And you're now a homicide detective? That's quite a jump."

"Less pay and worse hours, how could I resist?"

She chuckled just a little longer than she wanted to. "So what can I do for you, Detective?"

"I heard that you consult for law enforcement on arson investigations?"

"Used to consult. Now I just do defense."

"Prosecution to only defense? That's quite a jump."

She ignored the implicit question and said, "So I'm afraid you're out of luck, if you're looking to get a conviction."

"I'm not. My department's looking to blame the sixteen-year-old stepson of the victim who died in the fire. I think he's innocent, but the arson investigation doesn't support that."

She leaned forward on the desk. "Really? Well, now you have my attention."

Stanton unlocked his iPad and pulled up some photos. He accidentally closed the window and lost them then opened it again and handed it to her. "Sorry, just getting used to this thing. He died of smoke inhalation, but you can see the body's pretty damaged too. The arson investigator said there's a lot of evidence indicating that the fire was set intentionally. If that's true, I still don't think the stepson did it, but he was the only one around at the time."

"What's the matter? You don't trust a jury to acquit him?"

"No, absolutely not. Juries convict the innocent all the time."

She handed back the iPad. "Well, you're the first cop I've ever heard say that."

"I'm not a fool. Our system's not perfect. But I could really use your help. We don't have a lot of money, but I can probably get you approved for our standard consultation fees."

"If that kid gets life in prison, I guess there's no way I'd sleep at night if I turn down that offer. Okay, you've got me on board,

Detective. I have a space open this afternoon around four thirty, and I'd like to go see the house."

"So soon? It's not going anywhere."

"The sooner the better. Some of the evidence I'd be looking for dissipates over time. I know you send police escorts, but please, no more than one person. I like to work in some solitude."

"It'll just be me. Should I come pick you up?"

"I can meet you there if you leave the address with my receptionist."

He rose. "I really appreciate this, Emma."

"If he's really innocent, then it's my pleasure."

Stanton smiled and tapped the desk. "Thanks again. I'll see you down there."

CHAPTER 11

Sunlight came through the window in the kitchen and lit the room with a golden glow. Monique opened her eyes slightly and saw the warm light cascading over her bare legs. As a child, she would sit in the kitchen and play while her grandmother and aunt baked. The smell of pies and cookies was sometimes too much, and she would sneak cookies or piecrust when they weren't paying attention.

The house was quiet. She could hear quiet scratchings coming from the attic. She had always thought they had mice but could never find any evidence of them.

She was sitting on a chair. She tried to move her arms, but they wouldn't respond. She turned her head enough to take a quick look. Her forearms were tied to the arms of the chair with some sort of plastic wrap. Her ankles were tied also but not as tightly. The last thing she remembered was the feeling of suffocation, and she'd thought she was drowning before her head had hit the carpet and everything went black. And there was something else too... laughter. She remembered the echoing laughter that had come from behind her.

Glass clinked behind her, and she glanced back, toward her dining room. A man was sitting at the table, a linen napkin tucked into his shirt. He was handsome, and his head looked as though it had been shaved recently. He cut into a steak with a fork and knife and then dabbed at his lips with the napkin before taking a sip of red wine.

He noticed her looking at him, and smiled.

"Headache?"

She opened her eyes fully, taking him in. Then she immediately looked away. He needed to know that she couldn't identify him.

"Wha… what?" She felt lightheaded, as if she were floating in space.

"I said, do you have a headache?"

"Yes."

"I'll get you some aspirin." He finished his wine and rose, coming past her into the kitchen and stopping at the counter. "Um, which cupboard?"

"In the bathroom."

"Oh."

He left and came back a moment later. He filled a glass with water and held it in front of her with a couple of ibuprofen. She kept her eyes lowered, refusing to look at him. He giggled.

"Look at me."

"No."

"Why not?"

"I don't want to see you."

"Am I really that hideous? I apologize. I haven't seen a mirror in a long, long time." He opened her mouth gently and put the ibuprofen in and then put the glass to her lips. She drank a few sips and washed the pills down. "Oh… I see. You think if you don't see me I'll think you can't identify me to the police. Is that it?" She didn't answer. "But if I were going to kill you, identification wouldn't matter to me. Most sociopaths do what they do because it's an uncontrollable urge, like the pedophiles that grab a child in the grocery store in front of ten people. If I was that type of sociopath—which, given the circumstances, is a good assumption to make—it wouldn't matter one bit if you saw me or not. So please, open your eyes."

She squeezed them closed even tighter, the urge to scream and cry piercing her as she pulled her wrists up, trying to break the ties.

"Open your eyes, or I'll cut your eyelids off," he said, his voice flat and emotionless.

"No, please," she cried. "Please don't hurt me."

"Open your eyes."

Slowly, painfully, she opened them. The man knelt before her, the glass of water in his hands. He smiled as he stood up and put the glass on the counter.

"Are you hungry?" he said.

"There's money," she said. "My parents left a bunch of money here for emergencies. I'll give it to you if you let me go."

"Money, money money money. That seems to be the prime motivation for people today, yes? Although how the hell would I know? I've been locked in a room since I was a child. You hear that little rasp in my voice? I noticed that yesterday when I spoke to someone. It means my voice box has atrophied from disuse. I used to have a beautiful voice. I sang in a choir when I was young. But that's not what you're interested in."

"Please, please, just take whatever you want."

"Whatever I want? What if I wanted to rape you? Do you give me permission to do that? Then again, if you did, it wouldn't really be rape, would it?"

"Please," she cried, tears flowing down her cheeks now, "please don't hurt me."

"Hurt you, hurt you… now that is a good idea. I hadn't thought of that." He reached behind him and took a kitchen knife from a drawer. He brought it down to her breast and pressed the tip deep enough that it cut the skin. "Should I cut your tits off?"

"Please… please—"

He removed the knife, throwing it behind him without looking as he let out a sigh. "You know, I think you've really hit on something with this 'rape you and hurt you' stuff. Maybe we'll get to that later. For now, I'd like to finish my meal. You would be just shocked if you knew what swill I've been forced to eat these last years."

He walked into the living room and turned her stereo on. It was a classical station, and he returned to the kitchen and stopped. His eyes were fixed on a spot on the ceiling. "Anybody else live here?"

"No," she stammered.

"I disagree."

He smiled, his eyes refocusing on her, and blew her a kiss. Then he went back to the dining room and sat down, tucking the napkin back into his collar and taking a bite of steak as if she weren't there.

CHAPTER 12

Stanton heard the pounding on his door but didn't move. Maybe whoever it was would go away. One of the perks of living on the eleventh floor of a secure high-rise was that people couldn't drop in unannounced. He wondered who had made it past security without having to buzz.

The knocking got louder, and he pulled the covers up over his head, staring at a spot on the sheets, holding his breath, and waiting for the next knock. It didn't come for a long time, but when it did, he took a deep breath and rose to answer the door.

Stephen Gunn stood there with two coffees in his hand.

"What the fuck? It's, like, one o'clock. What're you still doin' in bed?"

"I just wanted to sleep in today."

"You been sleepin' in a lot these past few weeks," Gunn said, brushing past him into the apartment. He put the coffees down on the table. "Brought you some joe."

"Thanks," Stanton said, sitting down on the couch.

"Don't you want it?"

"No, I don't drink coffee, Stephen. You knew that."

"Oh, yeah, guess I forgot." Gunn came and sat down next to him. "Still gettin' used to the Mormon thing. Weren't any Mormons in East Brooklyn when I was growin' up, I can tell you that." He took a sip of coffee. "So what happened with that arson expert you were gonna bring in?"

"She cancelled because of some emergency. I'm meeting her at the Yazzies' house tomorrow afternoon."

"What's she look like?"

"Why does that matter?"

"Don't be a fag. Come on. What's she look like?"

"She's hot."

"No shit. How hot?"

"Out-of-your-league hot."

"Pss, you forget who you're talkin' to, son."

Stanton yawned. "She's too smart for you, Stephen. She wouldn't be interested."

"Yeah? And how the hell would you know?"

"Because I know. She wouldn't be interested."

"You, my friend, have never seen how attractive a bad boy is to shy nerdy types. I will bet you dinner I can get her to go out with me tonight."

"She might just do it out of pity. Although I think you'll be revolting enough to her that she won't even do that."

"Bet?"

"Sure."

"Okay, cool. Now get your ass dressed. We got a meetin'."

"With who?"

"CI. She's got some info on that homie we found in the dumpster."

"Michael Cisneros."

"Whatever. One junkie's just like the next to me."

Stanton went into the bathroom and started the shower. From his closet he took out jeans and a button-up shirt with a sports coat. "How'd you hear about this CI?" he shouted as he undressed and stepped into the shower.

"She called me. It was an old one I was usin' back in Narcs. They called her Super BJ Jones."

"Why?"

"Seriously?"

"Never mind."

"If you want, I could give you two some privacy, and you can find out why they called her that."

"I can do without gonorrhea, thanks."

"You can't get gonorrhea from a blow job, man."

"Of course you can. It can infect the throat and get passed to the genitals of another person."

"Well, I'm tellin' you, it'd be worth it with her. I had a sample back in my Narcs days, and Super Blow doesn't begin to describe it."

Stanton got out of the shower and toweled off. He was dressing in front of the mirror when he heard his fridge open and things being unwrapped. Then the balcony door slid open.

When he was done and went into the living room, he saw Gunn sitting on the railing of his balcony with his feet dangling over, eating a sandwich.

"This view, man. It's somethin' else. I don't know how you got this place on a cop's salary. If you was anybody else, I'd say you was takin' cream."

"I haven't stolen anything since I was sixteen years old, and even then I was terrible at it and got caught."

"What'd you steal?"

"Pack of condoms."

"You're kiddin'. Did you use 'em?"

"No. I just wanted some of the kids in gym to see them in my locker. I thought that might make me seem cooler."

"Did it work?"

"I didn't get a chance to find out, 'cause I got busted walking out of the store. That's what happens when you act like something you're not."

Gunn bit into the sandwich. "Yeah," he said quietly. "You ready?"

"You drive."

Stanton checked his watch. It had taken them thirty minutes to get to the freeway on-ramp. An accident somewhere ahead of them had so congested things that people were standing outside of their cars, talking.

"Shit. Super Blow ain't gonna wait forever." Gunn tapped the steering wheel with his index finger and then said, "Hang on to your balls."

He swung the car over to the shoulder, and one of the tires went up on the cement curb. He sped past the other cars and forced his way in between two SUVs. Horns blared, and Gunn hollered back at them as he wove out from between the SUVs and lightly bumped a car from behind.

"Pull over," Stanton said.

"They're fine."

"Stephen, pull over. We need to cover that damage."

"There was no damage, now pull your tampon out and relax."

Gunn reached the far shoulder and zipped past the other cars. If any of the other drivers opened their doors at any time, Gunn would ram right through it.

They reached the scene of the accident, and a uniform was standing there directing traffic. He was furious when he saw their car barreling toward him until Gunn held his badge up outside the window. The uniform immediately stopped other traffic and gave them an opening.

"Come on through, Detective," the officer shouted.

Gunn waved thanks as he whizzed past and into the open left-hand lane. He sped up to a hundred miles per hour and began shouting like a cowboy riding a bucking horse. Stanton watched him. Gunn laughed.

"You know what, Jon? You gotta get more fun outta life, man."

They took exit 239 to Palamino Street and found an old bar and grill named the *Ex-Wife's Place*. The exterior was brick and worn brown wood with neon beer signs in the windows. After they'd parked, Stanton checked his firearm's safety and stepped out of the car, following Gunn into the building.

The interior was as depressing as the exterior. It was dark and smelled of cigarettes and spilled beer. The only customers were a few drunks sipping away their hours at the bar. Stanton felt for them. They couldn't escape.

In the corner booth was a strikingly beautiful woman with chocolate skin and ruby-red lips. Her straight hair fell over her lean shoulders. She didn't fit in with this environment. Gunn sat across from her in the booth, and Stanton stood by, pretending to keep watch. CIs, particularly females, were jumpy and didn't talk freely in front of strangers.

"How you doin', sugar?" she said to Gunn.

"Good as can be. How 'bout you, Nicky? You gettin' by?"

"I'm always gettin' by, sugar. Just a matter of how well."

"You still with Pauly over there at Sherman Oaks?"

"Pssh, that broke-ass bitch couldn't keep a job, much less a woman such as The Nicole. I kicked his ass to the curb and sent him packin'."

There was a pause, and Stanton looked back and saw Gunn smiling.

"Is that what really happened?"

"Yes," she said. "Why? You don't believe me?"

"It's just weird 'cause I heard Pauly was doin' twenty for armed robbery."

She shrugged. "Well, I don't know about all that. All I know is I threw his ass out. I can't keep track of what he doin' when I ain't there."

"So no more Pauly. Who you got protectin' you now?"

She reached into her purse and brought out the handle of a pistol. "I got Mr. Browning watching my back."

"That's good. But you need someone out here watchin' your back, makin' sure you're not left alone with the sick fucks."

"I got my girls; I ain't need no man lookin' out for me." She rubbed his hand. "But you sweet for worryin' 'bout me."

"So what's the info you got for me on the body in the dumpster?"

"Cisneros? I was with this john the other night. We was in the Wal-Mart parkin' lot up there on Treemont, and he started talkin', right? I was blowin' him, and he just started talkin' and callin' me bitch and sayin' all sortsa crazy shit. Then he said, 'I'ma shank you like I shanked Mike's ass.' And he went off after that 'bout all the shit he was gonna do to me. Cuttin' me up and hangin' me, all sortsa ignorant shit."

"Did he try to hurt you?"

"No, he was just talkin'. Once he bust a nut he just paid me and be on his way. But I remember that 'cause I remember Cisneros was shanked."

"Yeah," Gunn said, "you could say that. He was stabbed over twenty times."

"Yeah, so I took down this dude's plate for you."

"Well, it could be nothin', but I'll take it. How much?"

"Six hundred."

"Shit, I ain't no rook out here tradin' blow jobs to not cite you, Nicky."

"Three hundred, then. I gots to pay my rent."

Gunn pulled out three hundred dollars from his wallet. "How's your son?"

"He good. He's in first grade now."

"No shit? Time just flies, huh?"

"Believe that," she said, taking the cash and stuffing it into her bra. She handed him a slip of paper with a license plate number on it.

Gunn rose. "If you need anything, you call me."

"I will, sugar. Thanks."

Gunn slapped Stanton's shoulder. "Let's go. We got a john to discuss his pillow talk with."

CHAPTER 13

Stanton sat in the passenger seat of Gunn's sedan while they called in to the precinct to run the plate number. The day was boiling hot, and he could feel sweat dripping down the back of his neck and soaking his collar. He turned on the air conditioning as Gunn finished his call.

"Tommy'll call us right back," Gunn said. "He's away from his desk, whatever the hell that means."

"He's probably having lunch."

"You hungry?"

"No."

Gunn waited a moment before saying, "So, the shrink. How was that?"

"What d'you mean?"

"Like, what'd you guys talk about, is it helpin', you know?"

"It's fine. I've been to a lot of psychiatrists. My dad was one, too. Whenever something happened at school, like I got into a fight or something, he thought it was a psychiatric emergency, and I would have to go to his office and take Rorschach tests."

"Man, I thought my old man was bad for givin' me beatings when he had one too many." His phone rang. "Hello?... Tommy, what, did you fall into the crapper?... Yeah, oh yeah?... Well, we can talk about that later. You got a hit for me?" Gunn grabbed a pen and started writing on his hand. "Uh huh... uh huh... got it. Thanks."

"Where is it?" Stanton asked.

"La Jolla. Maybe half an hour from here."

The freeway was relatively clear, and Gunn had the radio tuned to a rock station blaring death metal, which was giving Stanton a headache. He knew most of his headaches turned to migraines.

"You mind if we turn this off?"

"I guess," Gunn said. "So what kinda music you like?"

"Not this."

They rode in silence the rest of the way, and as they pulled off the La Jolla exit, Gunn folded a piece of gum into his mouth. They found the address in a residential area that was packed with apartment complexes and single family homes, all very middle-class—the cars, though not luxurious, were freshly washed and waxed, and the lawns were well maintained.

The house had a large tree in the front lawn and a minivan in the driveway. They sat looking into the house where a woman in a long-sleeved shirt and khaki pants vacuumed as two children ran around.

"You gotta be kiddin' me," Gunn said. "She musta given me a fake plate."

"I don't think so," Stanton said.

Stanton thought of the victim in this case, Michael Cisneros—a young homosexual male with no known gang affiliations or criminal history. Cisneros had only his mother, who was suffering from Alzheimer's and was unemployed. He was the type of victim a monster might think could disappear without anyone noticing.

"You tellin' me the dude who put twenty holes in Cisneros is married to fuckin' June Cleaver?"

"One or two wounds to major organs or the throat is enough to kill a person within minutes. When there are that many wounds, it's pure rage. It wouldn't be some drug dealer in the ghetto who got ripped off or something like that. They don't hide what they are. This person hides himself from the world."

"You can tell all that about our perp from some body in a

dumpster?"

"It's not just a random attack. Victims are always chosen, and they're chosen for a reason. Sometimes it's unconscious. When mass murderers are confronted with photos of all their victims, a lot of them are surprised how similar the victims all look. They didn't even realize they were driven to find a certain type of person."

Gunn waved his hand in a dismissive gesture. "Get the fuck outta here. Nicky fed me a bogus plate for cash. I've had CIs do it before."

"Cisneros's mother told us he was gay, right? And semen was found in the anal cavity during the autopsy."

"Yeah."

"Can you think of better cover for a bisexual psychopath than living in suburbia with a wife and kids?"

Gunn looked back at the house, watching the woman as she wound the electrical cord up and put the vacuum back in the closet. "I still say it's wrong."

"Only one way to find out."

Gunn exhaled. "You're gonna miss your arson investigator."

"We're not doing anything tonight, right? Just watch the house and get a sense for him when he comes home. We'll run his history and ask around about him before we pull him in."

"Ask around where?"

"Gay bars and clubs that Cisneros went to."

"Fuck. We just got off a stakeout. I hate this shit. It's bad for my bowels. I can only go at home."

"You'll be fine. Drop me off back at my place and call me as soon as he gets home."

Gunn pulled away from the curb, glancing one last time into the house.

CHAPTER 14

Stanton parked in front of the Yazzies' burnt-out home and turned off his engine. Some kids were playing nearby, and when they saw him they turned and walked away. He could see them drop the rocks in their hands onto the sidewalk. A house nearly burned to the ground and barely standing was simply too much of an enticement for them.

When he'd been a kid, a man had lived in a rundown house by a friend's apartment complex. Stanton and his friends would walk by every day on their way to a nearby soccer field or to the rec center. If they got near the yard, the man would sic his dog on them.

One day he'd tripped on the uneven sidewalk, and the dog got hold of his calf and wouldn't let go. The man stood over him and laughed and only pulled his dog off when neighbors began looking out their windows. Stanton's father tried to speak to the man to discuss what had occurred. Rather than calling the police or beating the guy to a pulp as any normal father would, he just knocked on his door and tried to discuss the situation. They spoke for a few minutes, and his father shook the man's hand.

He came back to Stanton and explained that Stanton wouldn't be going on the man's lawn anymore and that he was actually a nice fellow. He'd recently gotten a divorce. Stanton didn't hear any of it. The image of his father shaking hands with the man that had terrorized and wounded him cut so deeply that he never looked at his father the same way again. He didn't do it consciously or even want to, but he knew that was the day his connection with his father had been severed.

An FJ Cruiser came to a stop across the street, and Emma Lyon hopped out wearing jeans and a tight black shirt. She held a red case with a white handle and had a San Diego Fire Department badge issued by the county clipped to her belt. Stanton got out of the car and met her in the street.

"Detective, glad you came."

"To be honest, I haven't worked too many arsons before. I'm interested to see what you do."

"Same thing you do. Fire speaks to you. It tells you things, it breathes, it reproduces, it follows the easiest routes in a house. If you know what you're looking for, everything is right there. I'm guessing murders are the same."

"More or less. I do envy you one thing: no visiting the victims in the hospital."

"Yeah, I could never do that. I don't really want to know what people are capable of." She turned to the house and took a deep breath. "You ready?"

"After you."

Emma put down her kit on the front lawn and took out a small camera. She began taking photos of the house from all different angles as Stanton stood and watched. Then, as Benny had done, she diagrammed the house on graph paper. Without a word, she replaced the camera and the clipboard in her kit and went inside. Stanton followed. She paused at the doorway to put on latex gloves and run her hands over some burn impressions on the doors then began a room-to-room examination.

She spent the most time in the room the body had been found in. She measured burn marks on the walls and took photos of the puddle marks on the baseboards. She slowly went over every inch of flooring and would occasionally stop and snap a photo.

Stanton leaned against a chair in the bedroom that was covered with soot. He folded his arms, staring out the window as Emma finished what she was doing. After a long while, she stood up and turned to him.

"Fernando didn't do this."

"How can you tell?"

"The fire started here, probably from that portable heater that's been melted to the floor. There's something called flashover, it's a term of art in arson investigation. It's when the radiant heat in a room transforms it. Instead of a room with a fire in it, it becomes a room on fire—the point when the fire instantaneously gets out of control, almost a fireball. The fire shot up the wall, and then it was everywhere. Lower to the ground, it reached somewhere around eleven hundred degrees Fahrenheit. At flashover, the fire consumes every piece of fuel source in a room and then searches for more. It shot out of this room and down the hall. What we call puddle configurations can happen naturally from flashover because the fire's darting around everywhere."

"What about the spider web patterns on the broken glass?"

"That's more likely caused by rapid cooling than rapid heating. I read your arson investigator's report. The V marks he claimed indicated an accelerant also happen during flashover, whenever a new fuel source is ignited."

"How certain are you?"

"Ninety percent. I'll be a hundred percent after a few days in the lab. The only way to tell the difference between puddle configurations caused by accelerant and those caused by flashover is to analyze samples in the lab. I'll know in two days for sure, and I'll write a report and submit it to your office."

She began gathering samples into small circular dishes and then started packing up. They walked outside into the sunlight together, and Stanton stood next to her as she put her kit back in the car.

"I'll give you a call in two days, maybe less," she said, climbing in and starting the car. "Congratulations, Detective. You probably saved an innocent kid's life."

CHAPTER 15

Monique Gaspirini sat up in her bed. She had been moved to it by the man last night so that she could have access to her bathroom and sleep on an actual bed rather than the kitchen floor. The ties around her wrists had been removed, but her ankles were bound with a length of plastic he'd then knotted to the bed. She could get to the toilet, her television, and a few feet into the hall, but not to the window on the other side of the room.

Her alarm clock said 5:34 p.m., and she listened for exactly two minutes and didn't hear anything. Sometimes the man would leave for long times and not come back for hours. He would only leave at night and return at night. So far, he hadn't been here all day.

She fell to the floor and pulled on the plastic around her ankles. She had done it a hundred times and knew it was useless, but something drove her to pull on it with all her strength. She then looked at the knot that was looped several times around the frame of the bed. Monique grabbed one of her shoes and began pounding on the knot.

She struck it until sweat was pouring down her face and bits of shoe had flown over the floor. Exhausted, she leaned back against the bed, tucking her hair behind her ears. She curled up, her knees to her chest, and began to cry.

Not long after that she heard the back door open and then footsteps. Every single time it happened, she lost her breath, and her heart would pound so loudly in her ears that she was afraid it would explode.

The footsteps got louder and then went quiet; he was coming up the stairs. Her door opened, and the man stood there. He was wearing a suit now. He wore a white button-up shirt underneath with no tie. He was clean-shaven. There was an odd smell to him, like paint thinner or nail polish.

"Are you hungry?" he said.

She didn't respond.

"You know, it's hard for me to look after you if you don't—"

"Are you going to kill me?" she said, looking him in the eyes.

"Ah, it speaks. Am I going to kill you… What do you think?"

"I hear you laughing and talking to yourself at night. I thought there were two of you at first, but now I know that you talk to yourself.

I think you're crazy, and you're going to kill me."

He sat down in the chair against the wall and leaned forward on his elbows. "You're a very beautiful girl. Why no boyfriends coming over to check up on you? Oh, wait," he said, snapping his fingers. "Yes, yes he did."

She felt her heart sink into her stomach. "What did you do to him?" He laughed as he rose to leave the room. "What did you do to him? What did you do to him!"

The door slammed shut, and her scream echoed off the walls. She heard noises downstairs for a few minutes, and then a door opened and closed, and her car's engine started. She tried to stand up and watch it out the window but couldn't see that far. She collapsed onto her knees. She would've cried again, but no tears came.

CHAPTER 16

Stanton sat in the waiting area of his psychiatrist's office and read and reread an article about low-carb diets in a *Reader's Digest*. Eventually the door opened, and Jennifer motioned for Stanton to enter.

When he sat down, she poured herself a cup of water from a tray on her desk and offered some to him. He took it politely and drank a few sips.

"How have you been?" she said.

"Good."

"You have a little bit more stubble than when you came last. Are you growing a beard?"

"No, I just haven't shaved in a bit."

"So tell me what's going on in your life."

"Just the same old. We're working the case of a body that was found in a dumpster. My partner staked out the suspect's house and said he's a normal guy, nine to five with a wife and kids. He had a bunch of baseball equipment with him, and it turns out he coaches their little league."

"What did this man do?"

"He stabbed the victim, multiple times."

"Do you know why?"

"My partner thinks it's a drug deal gone bad."

"Is that what you think?"

"No. I think the murder displays rage. I think he's a closet homosexual who killed one of his lovers, maybe more than one, because of his inability to handle his sexuality."

"The first thing you said about him, Jon, was that he's normal. What did you mean by that?"

"Just what it sounds like—he's the guy who lives next door and comes to your barbeques and goes to basketball games. Things like that."

"Is that something that surprises you? That normal people can do horrible things?"

"No, not at all, actually. It did at first. But you arrest enough priests for pedophilia and enough cops for beating their wives, and you stop thinking that way."

"You haven't, though. The first thing that came to your mind when you thought of this man was that he was 'normal.' Do you feel like you're a normal guy?"

He leaned back in the chair. "No, not usually."

"Why not?"

"Probably because of what I do."

"Your job doesn't define you."

"I know that's what everybody says, but let's face it. It does. Cops, lawyers, doctors, professors, garbage men, engineers—they all have traits they share with their peers. Perhaps the job you have doesn't define you, but maybe your choice for going into it does."

"Assuming that's true, why would you think that you're not normal because you're a cop?"

"I don't think human beings were meant to see the suffering of other people as much as you see it in my profession. I see images and relive voices a lot, especially when it's quiet. That's why they say that the live ones are worse than the dead ones—the dead ones are quiet. That's why I asked for a transfer out of Sex Crimes to get back to Robbery-Homicide."

"You said you're not normal because of the things you see, but you also said that what you see doesn't affect you. I think those two statements are mutually exclusive."

"Maybe. I don't know. Cop logic, I guess."

She nodded and took a sip of water. "What else is going on in your life, outside of work? We didn't talk about any relationships you're in."

"I'm not in any right now. I was seeing a girl who lived in Las Vegas. Another cop. It didn't work out."

"What happened?"

"We already work crazy hours. Put long distance on top of that, and you've got a pen pal, not a relationship. One of us would've had to move."

"Did you discuss that at all?"

"Yeah. She didn't want to leave. After the case we had there, she got a promotion. It was a big chance for her. She'd always wanted to run a police department."

"Well, how about anyone else?"

"I haven't dated anyone since her. There is someone I'm considering asking out, though. She's a professor actually. Chemistry."

"That sounds like an interesting mix. The homicide detective and the chemistry professor."

"I don't even know if she's interested. I may not say anything."

"Do you like this person?"

"Yes. She's got a shy quirkiness about her that's appealing."

"Well then, what've you got to lose?"

He shrugged.

"Jon, I'd like to talk to you about something, and then I promise I won't bring it up again if you don't want to talk about it."

"Okay."

"Your partner, Eli Sherman. I hope you don't mind, but I Googled your name. I do that with all my patients. I read the articles about what happened. It seems like an incredibly traumatic event, and yet in the three sessions we've had, you haven't brought it up at all."

"I've dealt with it. As well as you can, I suppose."

"But this man was a close friend of yours, and he turned out to be strangling young women. That had to have caused an enormous amount of guilt."

"It did."

"Do you think that has something to do with your current issues?"

"It was a long time ago."

"Guilt isn't like a cut or a scrape, Jon. It doesn't just scab over and allow you to forget about it. It's more like an open wound, something that doesn't heal. It festers and grows. I've had numerous patients that commit horrible crimes and get away with them, at least for a time. I had a man once who raped a young girl while she was passed out drunk at a party. He opened up to me because of doctor-patient privilege. I saw him over the course of one year, and he absolutely fell apart. Eventually, he took his own life."

"I know what you're saying, but it's not something I can talk away. Eli Sherman—or whatever his name actually was—was a pure psychopath. One of the purest I've seen. Most psychopaths are self-destructive, and if they do turn criminal, they get caught because of their megalomania. Eli was caught because of a fluke—I happened to open his closet when he was in the shower. Otherwise, no one would've caught him. Deception is just what those personalities do. I have to accept that, and move on."

"Why did you say 'whatever his name actually was'?"

"He went by a lot of different names. The task force that was after him the year after his escape found that every name he had used was fake. They don't know his real identity."

"What was he like?"

"He had all of the traits I admired in a person. He was honest, loyal, tough… I never once saw him afraid of anything or unwilling to help somebody who needed it. When I found out what he really was… I think he had the ability to see what we look for in people, and knew those were the traits he needed to show me. Once the veneer was off, he was narcissistic and cowardly. Essentially the exact opposite of the man I knew." Stanton shifted in his seat and stared out the window a long time before speaking again. "I think he knew he could manipulate me right from the beginning."

"I only assumed you two were close because most police officers who come in here are closer to their partners than they are to their spouses. It sounds like you two actually had that type of relationship."

"We did. He'd call me at one in the morning if he was drunk at a bar, and I'd go pick him up. He'd come over for Sunday dinners… He knew I wouldn't go out to eat on Sundays, so every Sunday he would make a dish and bring it over and join my family for dinner. At the time I thought he was actually one of the best chefs I'd ever met, but now I'm thinking he probably picked it up on the way over." Stanton bit inside of his cheek and ran his tongue over the indentation. "I let him play with my children…" He took a deep breath. "But it doesn't matter now. My ex-wife is remarried, my children are growing up, and he's off in another country hiding in apartments and warehouses. It doesn't affect me anymore."

"I don't believe that for a second. I can even see it in your body language. You're more uncomfortable now than when we talked about a recent breakup." She leaned forward. "Jon, there's a group I have, of survivors, much like you. I'd like for you to come to our next session."

"What kind of survivors?"

"Well, one was married to a man who was a pedophile and hanged himself. Another is the mother of a gang leader who was executed."

"Oh, that kind of survivors. I don't think I would feel comfortable there right now."

"Well, when you're ready, I think it'd be incredibly beneficial for you to hear other people's stories. And you would really help them, as well. Some of them have tremendous anger toward the police, and I think you could really help turn that around. And it would make you realize you're not alone." She checked her watch. "Our half hour's almost up. Is there anything else you want to discuss with me right now?"

"No."

"How's the Xanax working?"

"Fine. I haven't had any of the serious side effects—just a stomachache the past couple of days."

"That should go away on its own. If it doesn't, please don't hesitate to call me."

He rose. "I won't. Thanks, Doc."

"You're welcome. I'll see you next week. And Jon, please consider coming to that group."

Stanton nodded and went out the door without saying anything else. When he got to his car, he had to sit a moment and calm his breathing before he started the engine and pulled away.

CHAPTER 17

Several young girls sat in a car on the corner of Thirty-Third Street in Logan Heights, one of them holding cash out the window. Several cars drove by and could see exactly what was happening as the girl handed the cash over to a man in orange shorts. He had prison tattoos over his arms and shoulders. The man whistled, and a boy of about twelve ran into an alleyway and came back out with a small plastic baggie. He handed it to the girls, blew them a kiss, and then ran back to the alley.

Detective Stephen Gunn watched this from his car as he finished his cigar and threw it out on the sidewalk. He got out of the car and dodged traffic crossing the street. As he approached the girls, he could see the man with the tattoos leaning against the driver's door, a smile on his face now. Gunn could hear their conversation.

"You girls suck dick?" the man asked.

One of the girls giggled. "No."

"That's bullshit. I know y'all suck dick. Why don't we hit my apartment and smoke some weed and you can show me how you suck that dick?"

Gunn came up behind him, grabbed him by his head, and slammed him nose first into the car. The man swore and instinctively reached for the Glock tucked into his waistband. Gunn got there first, emptied the round from the chamber, and threw the weapon over by a garbage can.

Gunn held up his badge to the girls. "Unless you want to be suckin' his dick while you're in jail, I suggest you get the hell outta here." They started the car. "And girls, I'll be takin' that crystal you just bought… thank you. *Now* get the hell outta here." Gunn pushed the man away as the girls drove off.

Blood was pouring out of the man's nose. "You broke my fuckin' nose."

"How you been, Juan? You know, it's funny, I'm sittin' there today hard at work and I realize, you know what? I haven't heard from my good pal Juan in almost three weeks. Imagine that, man. I ain't heard from you in three weeks."

"Yo, I been sick, man. I just got back out here on dese corners, man."

"Yeah? 'Cause I drove by here couple days ago and saw you hangin' out with your faggot friend over there."

"Yeah, I been back for a few, but I been outta the game for a minute."

Gunn glanced around. "Where's my fuckin' money, Juan?"

"I told you man, I been outta the game. I ain't got no money."

"Really? You ain't got no money, huh?" Gunn took a few steps toward him and Juan jumped back. "You old school, Juan, right? You always talkin' about how life was back in the day. I mean you're only like, what? Thirty-five? But since all you wet-back gangsters die out here at twenty, that's pretty old to still be in the game, right?"

Gunn lunged at him and grabbed him by the throat. He dragged him close enough to smell his breath and look into his eyes.

"Here's a rule you can fuckin' remember: this is my corner. This ain't your corner, it ain't the LHG's corner. This is my corner, and I call the fuckin' shots. Now you pay me what you owe me or we got a big problem, you and me, and maybe that butt-buddy of yours over there gets a little promotion 'cause his boss is missin' in action."

"I'll get you the money, man. I ain't playin'. I'll get it to you. I need some time, though, man. I just got back in the game, man. I wasn't lyin'."

"You got three days to get me three weeks' worth of payments."

"Three days? Man, I can't do that. I can't sell fast enough, man."

"Well, then you better rob a fuckin' truck or take out a loan or something 'cause either my money or your balls are goin' home with me in three days."

"All right, man, all right. I'll find it. I'll find it."

Gunn let him go. "See, I knew you were reasonable. That's why I like you, Juan. Reasonable."

As Gunn got back into his car, he saw Juan go and pick up his firearm from near the garbage. Juan stared at him with venom but only tucked the gun into his pants and went back to work.

It was nearly six in the evening when Lieutenant Daniel Childs stopped by Jonathan Stanton's office and leaned against the doorframe. He had found conversations with his detectives went a lot faster, saving him more time, when he didn't sit down or come in.

Stanton sat at his desk, busy at his computer. Childs watched him. He was researching something about homosexual sadists—a study that, from what Childs could tell, was conducted almost fifty years ago.

"You're the only detective I know who does research the way you do."

"Most crimes are solved by snitching. The type I specialize in isn't. Sometimes even *they* don't know they're doing it." He turned and faced Childs, putting his feet up on the desk. "Gotta take every advantage I have."

Childs took a few steps into the room so he could read the screen. "'Schizo-Affective Disorders in Homosexual Psychopathy.' I prefer *Sports Illustrated*, myself."

"This study was conducted in the sixties, and it's spooky how accurate they were. These people, like the one I think we're seeking for Cisneros, are incapable of happiness. They want to impose their own misery on everybody else. This guy we're after, he has a family. I bet everyone in the community thinks they seem like the perfect family, but at home he's probably a Vlad Dracula. I wouldn't be surprised if he tortures his children as a form of discipline."

"You one dark motherfucker, Jon. You need to bowl or play tennis or whatever white people do to clear your head."

"I'm all right."

"How's the dating situation goin'?"

"I'm okay, really, Danny, you don't need to worry about me. I was actually just debating whether to ask out somebody I met."

"Oh yeah?" Childs said, sitting down. "Who is she?"

"The arson investigator we hired."

"Well, call her."

"Maybe later."

"No, no, this is a direct order, man. Call her right now while I listen, and ask her to dinner and a movie or whatever the hell Mormons do for fun. Ice cream, whatever."

"I really don't think—"

"I ain't kiddin'. Direct order. Call her."

"All right, fine. Hang on." He pulled out his phone and pulled her up in his contacts.

"She in your contacts already? This is serious."

Stanton smiled as the phone rang. Emma answered on the third ring.

"This is Emma."

"Hey, Emma, it's Jon. Stanton. From the SDPD. We worked—"

"Of course I remember you, Jon. What's up?"

"Hey, um, I was just wondering if—"

"You're probably calling about the samples. They're not done yet. The labs that I trust take about—"

"No, I wasn't calling about that. I was calling about something else. Um." He looked at Childs, who made a motion of sticking his finger in a hole. Stanton had to suppress a laugh. "I was just wondering if, um, you'd like to grab dinner some time? With me. Grab dinner with me."

"Oh, well… yeah, why not?"

"Okay, how about Friday?"

"Friday's no good. I've got a symposium on ion-selective electrodes."

Childs whispered, "Oh, man, beaten out by an electrode."

"Well," Stanton said, "how about Saturday?"

"Let me check… yeah, that should be fine. Should I come pick you up? Or, well, I don't know. Do you want to meet there?"

"Sure. I'll just text you the address."

"Sounds good. See you then."

"See you."

Childs busted up laughing. "Oh, man. Nothing better than two nerds trying to flirt."

"She's not one of your strippers, that's for sure."

"My strippers are top-quality American beef, Brother Stanton. You should try one sometime. Might loosen you up a bit and get you to stop thinking about homosexual schizophrenic-whatevers torturing their kids." He stood up. "Much respect, Jon. That took balls, I know."

"Thanks."

As Childs left, Stanton looked at his phone. He dictated his date into his phone and smiled as he saw it appear on his calendar.

CHAPTER 18

Jesse Brichard finished his shift and found his sedan in the airport parking lot. He sat in the car for a moment and then took out the silver flask from the glove compartment and threw back a few swallows, spilling a few drops on his pilot's uniform.

He remembered why he'd wanted to be a pilot: the idea of freedom. The bastards could take your house and car, your money… but they couldn't take the air. His father had been a pilot and his father before him. It was a family tradition. But with each successive generation, the pay and benefits had shrunk to the point that he now worked a second full-time job just to support his family. He could make more managing a fast-food restaurant than he could making sure three hundred people landed safely and got home to their families.

Ah, to hell with it. Maybe they'll just replace me with robots.

He started the car and pulled away and before long was on Interstate 5 heading home to his family in Claremont. The salty ocean air was warm as evening fell, and he enjoyed the tang of it on his tongue. He turned on the oldies station, and the Moody Blues' "Nights in White Satin" was playing.

He got home and pulled into his garage. His wife's truck was already there, and he took another swig of the beer in his hand and headed inside. His two boys, Hank and Dover, sprinted past him, Dover yelling something about Hank stealing the last orange juice.

"Hello to you too, boys," Jesse said.

His wife stood in the kitchen, stirring a bowl of fruit and whipped cream to top an angel food cake. Jesse went over and stuck his finger in the bowl and came away with a big gob that he promptly stuck in his mouth.

"Wait till it's done," his wife said.

"What? No hello from you, either?"

She leaned in and gave him a quick kiss on the lips. "How was your day?"

"Shit, but what're you gonna do?" he said, going to the fridge and getting a bottle of beer.

"Jess, I've told you about that language in front of the boys."

"Sorry, sorry. It's just Molly. She won't let up. Today she told me—*me*—that my uniforms are too wrinkled, and if I want to keep flying her planes I need to look professional. She's like twenty, and she's my boss 'cause she has some fucking degree?"

"Jess, the language."

"I'm sorry, but I get upset about this." He popped open the beer and took a long swig. "What'd you guys do today?"

"Nothing much. When the boys came home from school, I took a nap and they played video games."

"Those damn games. You didn't have those when I was kid, and you actually had to go out and play with other kids."

She shrugged and went to the oven.

Jesse went into the living room and lay down as his boys ran up the stairs. He turned on the television and watched a random show on HBO as night fell outside.

Jesse Brichard didn't usually dream, so it was odd when he heard voices. There was a male voice, calm and rusty, almost as though it had a grain to it. His wife was crying and begging, and the man was speaking to her softly. He'd heard this conversation before. His own father was a boozer: beer with breakfast and lunch and hard liquor for dinner, sometimes on top of coming home drunk from the bar. He remembered nights of his mother crying and him in the next room listening, hoping that they would stop fighting long enough to remember that they loved each other.

The hairs on the back of his neck stood, and Jesse was awakened by the impression that someone was watching him.

He opened his eyes.

Above him stood a man: bald and wearing a nicely cut Italian suit. He was handsome, or at least what would be considered handsome, except for his greasy-looking skin and the thick forest of stubble on his cheeks and chin. The man smiled and tilted his head, like a dog observing something amusing.

"Hi, Jesse. Bye, Jesse."

The last thing Jesse felt was the thick metal hammer slamming into the top of his skull.

CHAPTER 19

Ocean Beach Park was nearly empty this early in the morning as the sun came up and roasted the sky a bright orange and pink. A couple of joggers were out, a few people walking dogs, but the majority of the dozen or so people there were surfers. They were like a primitive tribe with their own language, their own customs, and violently opposed to outsiders. In the fifties and sixties, even the police tolerated assaults against tourists if they happened in known local surfing spots.

For the surfers, there was a spiritual aspect to surfing that made it different from everything else—not just sports, but everything. It was communing with nature by submitting to its will. Surfers were at the mercy of the ocean, and if it chose to do so that day, it would show them the majesty of creation. And if it chose to that day, it would take their lives as payment for their trespass.

Many of the surfers were rebellious youth. Religion and regular church attendance were not parts of their lives. This, enveloping oneself in nature, was their form of worship. Nature demanded respect and nothing but the highest standards, from both the surfers and those on the beach observing. But like everything else, standards had deteriorated.

Of the new generation of surfers, nearly half were drug addicts, and half were maniacs. Fights were common, as was drug use on the beach, which led to near-drowning in the sea. Despite this, some had faith in the ocean and saw surfing as those early surfers had, as if they were descendants of some great ancestors from long ago. They were fewer and didn't come out when the beaches were packed with valley youth and tourists, but they were there.

Jon Stanton belonged to this latter group.

He waxed his board and zipped up his wetsuit. The sand, just beginning to warm, felt silky as it ran between his toes. He stood and listened to the waves crackle against the shore before picking up his board and going in.

The water was cool, almost cold. He sat quietly and adjusted and then paddled out. When he was far enough, he turned toward shore, and waited for his set.

The waves were low at first, but as time went by, they grew. Eventually, all the surfers who had been asleep in their cars or lying on beach towels filled the water. They dotted the massive waves like seals fleeing some predator, zipping back and forth and taking massive falls as their boards flew in one direction and they flew in another.

Stanton hit his stride on one wave in particular. He was steady during the smooth ride. He pointed his toes over the board and stood straight, as if the wave were a regal caravan carrying him back to shore. It lasted only thirty or so seconds, but it felt like years. He thought of his children, his two sons that he hadn't seen in months, and wondered whether they thought about him anymore. He tried so hard to see them and to be their father, but he knew his ex-wife was pouring poison in their ears. His sons saw him out of an obligation, some duty they'd learned at school, but they had turned to their stepfather for the guidance and love Stanton was supposed to provide.

Back on shore after a good hour, he lay down on his towel. The sun was bright and hot now, and it felt good against his face. A shadow suddenly blocked it, and he looked up to see Billy Sakamoto zipping up his suit.

"You're still wearing your badge," Stanton told him.

"Oh." Billy looked down at the detective shield around his neck and slipped it off. "You goin' back in?"

"Not for a while. I'll hold it."

Billy tossed it to him and finished zipping up. "I'm actually glad I ran into you, Jon. How are you and your new partner doing?"

"Fine."

"Stephen's been treating you good?"

"Yeah. Why?"

"Any reason they put you two together? At least, any reason they told you?"

"No. They just said it was a random pairing."

"Hm. It could be, I guess. Did you know his last three partners asked for transfers or new assignments?"

"I didn't know that."

"Stephen's got a reputation. He's kinda crazy, Jon. One of his partners was Jensen over in Missing Persons. You should talk to him. He told me Stephen once beat the shit outta this perp they were interrogating 'cause he wouldn't tell them where the kid he'd snatched was. The guy had to go to the hospital afterwards. Stephen had broken a bunch of the guy's bones and fractured his skull."

Stanton shrugged. "Sounds like a product of the rumor mill."

"Maybe. Just watch your back is all I'm saying. Partnerships are like marriages. What happens to him happens to you, and what he does, you do."

"I appreciate it, Billy. Thanks."

Billy nodded and then headed for the sea as Stanton lay back, letting the sun cook his face and dry his wet skin.

Nearly an hour later Billy came out, got his badge, and said goodbye. Stanton had fallen asleep.

He rose and stretched before gathering up his towel and checking his phone. Childs had left a message.

Call me back.

Stanton dialed his number.

"Jon, where you at?"

"I'll be heading in after a shower. What's up?"

"We got something for you and Gunn. Another arson."

"What about Sell and Wharton? They just cleared two of their cases."

"You too busy?"

"No, it's just that arsons aren't really my thing. I think Wharton used to be a firefighter."

"This is… this is something else. I want you on it. Drop everything else and come down. Gunn's already on his way."

"All right, text me the address."

As Stanton got into his car, he received a text message. He thought it was the address, but then he received another one. One was the address from Childs, and the other text came from Gunn:

Already down here. Pretty bad. Sick fuck killed a whole family.

CHAPTER 20

Stanton stopped in front of the home. Several firefighters were walking around, their faces covered with dark soot. A group on the lawn passed around a jug of water, and Gunn stood with them. He wasn't laughing or cracking jokes as he usually did around a macho crowd. All of them looked sullen and angry.

As Stanton walked up, Gunn said something to the firefighters, and they nodded. He walked over to Stanton and shook his head.

"Fucking bastard," Gunn said, looking at the charred remains of what had once been a house.

The entire frame had burned to the ground. Only the chimney remained, and, oddly enough, part of the front door's frame.

"How many?" Stanton asked.

"Whole damn family, parents and two kids. They're tied up in the middle of what we think was the living room."

"I need to see it."

Finding one of the forensic techs, they got two pairs of sterile booties and stretched them over their shoes. Stanton snapped on latex gloves and a mask over his mouth and nose. They entered the house through what had been the wall next to the front door. Stanton could see furniture melted to the floors. Every inch of carpet had burned away, and the fire had gotten down to bare cement, since there was no basement.

Up what Stanton guessed was once a hallway rested a mass of charred remains. Two forensic techs snapped photos and took measurements of various angles in the room. Benny, the arson investigator, was standing behind them, watching.

"Get him out of here," Stanton said to Gunn.

Gunn didn't ask for a reason. He walked over to Benny and whispered something in his ear. Benny said, "What? What the hell for?" Gunn whispered again, and Benny packed up his gear and left.

"I hope you got another arson investigator 'cause I ain't got no idea what I'm lookin' at," Gunn said, returning.

"Yeah, I texted her on the way down. She should be calling me."

"Oh, your little filly, huh? Trying to pad her hours a bit?"

"She didn't charge us for last time. I don't think she cares about money. Do we have IDs yet?"

"Yeah," Gunn said, taking out his phone. "Jesse and Darlene Brichard. Their two boys, ten and twelve. He's an airline pilot, and she's a stay-at-home mom. Neighbors said they're a good family. No shady people ever comin' over or nothin' like that. Pulled their criminal histories, nothing but a few speeding tickets."

Stanton walked over to one of the forensic techs standing over the bodies. He was holding a camera and trying to snap a photo of some teeth on one of the corpses.

"Jon, Stephen," the tech said without looking up from what he was doing, "how are you guys?"

"Better than these poor bastards," Gunn said.

"That's the understatement of the year."

"Fuck me, you CSIs always have to be such fucking nerds?"

"Matty," Stanton interrupted, "we need to preserve everything for the arson investigator. Don't let the ME's guys take the bodies until she has a look."

"Not sure I can help you with that, Detective. These bodies are barely held together. I've never seen a house fire burn so hot. It was like an incinerator in here. Even some of the bones are little more than ash. Big ones—the tibia and fibula, spine—they're still there, but all the bones in the hands and feet are done. The two little ones might break down and go with the wind any second. I've never seen a fire so hot."

"You already said that," Gunn said, annoyed. "Just do your best and don't fuck anythin' up until Jon's girlfriend gets here."

Stanton ignored him and leaned down. The bodies were burned to an absolute black. On many burn victims, patches of flesh color remained, or at least the red muscle exposed where skin had been seared away. Nothing like that remained with these victims. They were burned so thoroughly that there wasn't a single inch of flesh that hadn't turned to ash. He had never seen anything like it.

"Any of the neighbors see anything?"

Gunn shrugged. "We canvassed up and down, but not that many people are home from work yet. We'll try again tonight; see if anyone saw anything when they was heading out to work this morning."

Stanton's phone rang: Emma.

"Hey."

"Hey, Jon. I got your text. Look, I'm sorry, but I only did that one favor for you guys to help out that kid. I can't come to your scene."

"I've never even heard of anything like this, Emma. Even the bones have turned to ash. The fire must've been two or three thousand degrees. How can a fire burn that hot?"

"Specific spots in flashpoints can certainly get up that high. I've never heard of an entire house reaching that temperature, though. The victim must've been close to a fuel source during flashpoint."

"Victims. They're bound with chain. It's melted, but I can see remnants on the ground surrounding them."

"I'm sorry to hear that. But I can't help you. I've told you before, I don't work with law enforcement."

"Could you just come supervise our guy and make sure he doesn't screw it up?"

"Sorry, Jon. But if he nails the wrong suspect again, I will testify for the defense about his incompetence. In fact, I've contacted the fire marshal. He shouldn't be investigating fires anymore."

"Let me guess. The fire marshal's assistant said they'll get the message to him and give you a call back, but so far no one's contacted you?"

"That's just normal—"

"Yes, it is normal. And your complaint went into a trash bin. Benny's going to retire on this job and when he leaves, he'll pick his successor, who'll be just as bad as he is. That's how government works.

I'm asking for your help."

"I know, and you have no idea how much I would like to help you. But I can't. I'm sorry. I understand if you want to cancel our date."

"No," Stanton said, "no, our work shouldn't interfere with that. I'll call you later."

"Okay, bye."

Gunn said, "No go, huh?"

"Get Benny back here. But don't let him out of your sight for a second."

CHAPTER 21

Two days after Stanton left the fire site of the Brichards' home, he didn't have anything more than he'd had when he'd arrived at the scene. He had spoken with a dozen neighbors, and none of them had seen or heard anything. No family members could identify any trouble between the couple, and no one hinted that it might have been a murder-suicide.

As he got on the freeway, he received a text from Gunn asking if he wanted to hit a couple of the clubs Cisneros had frequented. Spending his time at the city's gay clubs wasn't how he'd expected his Friday night to go, but he agreed.

He picked Gunn up at an apartment complex he hadn't been to before. Gunn was sitting on the steps, smoking, and he threw his cigarette on the ground when he saw Stanton and then looked up and said something to a woman sitting on her balcony on the building's top floor.

"Who was that?" Stanton asked.

Gunn leaned the seat back and rolled down his window. "Just a piece of ass. I talked to Cisneros's mom again. She gave me a list of the three clubs he most liked to go to."

"He told his mom what gay clubs he liked?"

"Hey, some parents are more progressive than others. My old man woulda put my head through a wall. Different strokes for different folks."

Stanton put the name of the first club, Playland, into his GPS. It was on Fourth Avenue not far away. The building had once been a warehouse and was now surrounded by parking lots. Stanton saw a homeless shelter down the block, and even though night had fallen, the line went around the corner—people waiting for any amount of food left over from the five o'clock dinner. Many of them looked no more than eighteen or nineteen.

"What d'ya think makes these kids wanna live on the streets?" Gunn asked.

"Some of them are drug addicts, and it's easier to live on the street than try to maintain a job. Some of them are mentally ill, and the institutions are full… A lot of 'em come from abusive homes, and the streets are better."

"With all the sick fucks we got out here? These kids don't know what they're doin'. They need a good kick in the ass is what they need."

Stanton parked in front of the club. It wasn't obvious exactly how you got into the building, and they had to look for the entrance. He saw a ramp leading to what looked like an underground garage, and they followed it to large black double doors. Stanton could hear voices inside, and he pounded on it with his palm. After a few seconds, an Asian man in a tight black shirt answered.

"Yeah?"

Stanton flashed his badge. "We need to talk to the manager."

"Which one?"

"Whoever is here the most and would recognize a regular."

"I don't have to let you in without a warrant."

Gunn cut in. "Look, shithead, don't make me bust your fuckin' head open and come in there. I'm sure I'm gonna find some coke, probably some illegal porn, maybe a gun or two—though I know you fags don't like the feel of a real man's gun in your hand."

"Fuck you."

Before Stanton could stop him, Gunn grabbed the man by the throat and slammed his head into the door. The man fought back, and

Gunn took out an extendable baton from his belt, snapped it opened, and whacked the guy on the head twice before he grabbed his hand, pressed it on the door, and crushed two of his fingers with the baton. It happened so quickly Stanton couldn't even respond.

The man was screaming as Stanton shoved Gunn away and stepped between them so Gunn couldn't strike him again. "What's the matter with you?" Stanton shouted at Gunn.

Gunn ignored him and yelled, "Tommy Chang, you gonna have to fist your boyfriend with your left hand now."

A woman in a sparkling tank top came out from behind the door. Her long blonde hair was pulled back, and her eyes went down to the badge clipped to Gunn's hip. She called for someone to help her, and they lifted the man off the ground and helped him inside.

"Take him to the emergency room," she said calmly before stepping outside and shutting the door behind her. "I'm Shannon Gunther, the manager. Can I help you?" she asked Stanton.

"I'm sorry about your employee. We can pay for his ER visit, and I'm sure the county can set him up for any lost wages."

"I know how you cops are. If I were to sue the county next week, my club would be raided and drugs would just happen to be found everywhere. So just tell me what you want and be on your way."

Gunn pulled out a photo of Cisneros. "You know this guy?"

"Yeah, that's Mikey. I haven't seen him in a long time, though."

"He's dead," Gunn said. "His body was found with twenty air holes poked into it."

Stanton said, "When was the last time you saw him?"

"Two weeks ago, maybe. He liked coming here every Friday for hip-hop night."

"Did you see him leave with anybody that night?"

"Officer, everyone here leaves with somebody. I don't keep track. I'm sorry he was killed. I liked him. But hundreds of people come through here on the weekends. I don't think I can help you. Try the Trap Door, though. That's where he was on Saturday nights. Now if you'll excuse me, I need to find a bouncer. Looks like we're gonna be one short tonight," she said, looking at Gunn.

When she had gone back inside, Stanton turned to Gunn.

"You were out of line. You do that again, and I'll have to go to Childs."

"Fuck him. My cousin died of AIDS, and these queers were the ones who brought it here."

"That man never did anything to you, and the manager knows more than she's telling us, but she doesn't want to help us now."

Gunn threw his hands in the air and turned toward the car. Stanton followed, and they drove in silence, heading down University Avenue and to the Trap Door.

The club also shared a wall with a restaurant open until midnight. Both were designed in blacks and golds. Couches and beds were throughout the space, and the front wall was just glass, allowing those walking by to look in on what was happening.

Stanton went inside. Gunn appeared agitated. He was fidgeting as they sat down in the waiting area near the hostess podium.

"How many?" the hostess said to Stanton without looking up.

"I actually need to talk to the night manager of the restaurant and the manager of the club."

"Can I tell him what you need?"

Stanton held up his badge. Without a word, the girl went to the back of the room behind a bar where a man in a turtleneck with wire-frame glasses was doing an inventory of the liquor. He saw Stanton and swore under his breath as he walked over.

"What can I do for you, Officer? I promise our liquor license is in order and there's no—"

"I'm not from the state." He pulled out a picture of Cisneros. "Do you recognize this man?"

"No."

"You didn't even look at the picture. Please take a look."

He sighed and then looked at the photo. "No."

"He was murdered," Gunn said loudly. "You sure you don't recognize him?"

"Don't recognize him. Sorry. Can I go now?"

Gunn stood up and Stanton stepped in front of him. Their eyes met, and for a moment neither one of them said anything.

"Get outta my way," Gunn said.

"I can smell the whiskey on your breath. You shouldn't be on duty."

"I said, get outta my way."

Stanton hesitated, and then stepped to the side. Gunn walked toward the manager when Stanton said, "If you touch him, you're under arrest."

Gunn laughed. He turned to Stanton, and the two squared off again. The manager quietly sneaked away.

"You don't have the balls."

"Go home, Stephen. I'll cover the rest of the night."

Gunn lit a cigarette. He took a long puff and then blew smoke in Stanton's face. "You know what? I'm gonna have dinner here, and then I'm callin' a cab. Why don't you just go back to your empty apartment and read your damn books? No wonder your wife left you." Gunn turned toward the waitress. "Party of one."

Stanton watched as Gunn was seated. He began flirting with a table full of middle-aged women next to him. Stanton left the restaurant. The night air was cool, and the moon was a bright crescent in the sky. He pulled out his phone and got the address for Playland again before glancing inside the restaurant to see a waitress place a wine bottle on Gunn's table.

CHAPTER 22

Later in the evening after doing some paperwork, Stanton drove to Playland with the windows down, enjoying the breeze. He thought about the charred remains of what had once been a family. They hadn't appeared human. It reminded him of the ashen shells he'd seen at Vesuvius when he'd traveled to Italy as a graduate student for a summer.

He waited in his car for a while and read the Brichard file Gunn had uploaded onto the SDPD server. There were no outstanding debts other than some student loans Jesse Brichard still had with UNLV for his bachelor's degree. Neither Jesse nor his wife Darlene had a criminal record, and neither one had ever called the police on the other.

Stanton flipped through the preliminary report from the Medical Examiner's Office. The bodies had been so fragile they'd crumbled when an attempt was made to move them. Almost no physical evidence was gathered; everything biological had been burned away in the fire, except their teeth. Stanton regretted that they wouldn't be able to tell if Darlene had been sexually assaulted. There was a massive difference between the motivations of someone who sexually assaulted her before her death and someone who just lit them on fire to watch their suffering. He also couldn't rule out a crime of opportunity: someone broke in for a routine burglary, discovered the family was still home, and had to deal with them.

A slight tinge of resentment tugged at his gut. This was the case he should be working right now, not Cisneros. He had a feeling that the person who killed Michael Cisneros was not as immediately dangerous as the man who'd lit the fire. Gunn should've been at this club following up.

Stanton closed the file and stepped out of the car. He walked down to the main entrance and the large black doors. One door was open. There was a large man with tattoos on his neck and arms standing in front of the door, and a line had formed to one side of a velvet rope in front of him. Another bouncer sat on a stool with a list in his hand, letting in the VIPs.

Stanton flashed his badge, and they let him through without a word. The interior of the club was beautifully decorated in silvers, reds and blacks. The dance floor wasn't far from the entrance, and though it wasn't yet late, it was packed with drunks and those on ecstasy and other stimulants. Many of them would be dancing until five or six in the morning when they would go home to sleep, wake up in the evening, and head out to the clubs again for Saturday night.

He saw Shannon behind the bar, and he pushed his way through the crowd to get there. One man whispered something in his ear and wrapped his arm around Stanton's waist, and Stanton removed the guy's arm and kept walking.

"Back for more?" Shannon said when she saw him. "I can't spare any other employees to the hospital."

"I'm sorry. That shouldn't have happened."

"He's got a fractured skull. He's thinking about suing the county."

"He should."

"Do you really think he should?"

He hesitated. "No."

"I knew I liked you," she said. "Vice would be in here every night looking for any excuse to close me down, wouldn't they?"

"Yes."

She shook her head. "I gotta give it to you cops. You're one hell of an organized gang."

"We're just a reflection of the society we live in."

She took a shot of tequila that was offered to her by a woman on the other side of the bar. "So what can I do for you... is it Detective?"

"Just call me Jon."

"What is it you need?"

"I want to talk to you about Michael Cisneros."

"I already told you everything I know."

"We both know that's a lie."

A slight smile parted her lips as she reached under the bar and came up with a slice of lime. She gently sucked on it before throwing it in a nearby trash bin. "Follow me."

She walked around the bar to the dance floor, and Stanton followed. The crowd was packed together, and the smell of marijuana and cologne hit him like an invisible wall. The music was too loud to speak over, so Stanton just stayed close to Shannon as she slid in between the moving bodies like a snake.

On the far side of the dance floor they reached a padded door with a bouncer in front; he opened the door for them and they stepped through.

The room was nearly soundproof, and the only thing they heard from outside was a low thud from the bass. The room was decorated entirely in crimson—all the chairs, the couches, and even the bar. Most of the people here were in couples, and two women were making out on one of the couches. Shannon grabbed two drinks from the bar with one hand and sat down next to the women, running her other hand over the thigh of one of them.

"This is Donna. She's my partner. Have a seat."

Stanton sat next to her. "You knew Mike better than you let on."

She tried to hand one of the drinks to Stanton, but he turned it down. "Suit yourself." She guzzled one and then leaned back on the couch, sipping the other. "He would housesit for me whenever I left town. Sometimes I'd hire him to tend bar when he was broke and needed cash. He was a good kid. His mother's ill, and he stayed home to take care of her rather than get his own place."

"Did you ever see him with anyone who hasn't been back since?"

"Yeah, there's someone." She lifted the other drink. "But first you gotta take a drink," she said, with a mischievous smile.

Stanton pulled out his handcuffs and snapped them on her wrists. Standing her up, he said, "Shannon Gunther, you are under arrest for obstruction of justice in the homicide investigation of Michael

Cisneros. You have the right to remain silent. Should you choose to waive that right, anything you say can and will—"

"Easy, easy, I was just playing. I'll help you."

Stanton removed the cuffs. "No games. I want a name right now."

"We called him Big Harry. His first name was Henry. I don't know what his last name was. Honestly, I don't."

"Would you recognize him in a photo line-up?"

"Yes."

"Who is he?"

"He's a meal ticket."

"What does that mean?"

"He's an older guy who buys things for his younger lovers. Takes care of them. He bought Mikey a new watch last month."

"Do you have any information about where he lives or what he does?"

"We don't scan IDs in the VIP section. Not yet, anyway. But I think Mikey mentioned once that he was a pharmacist."

"What else do you know about him?"

"That's it. Other than he likes younger men, but he's bisexual."

Stanton glanced around and noticed that the room was filling up now. Couples were making out on couches and in the two canopied beds that took up the corner. Drinks were served to them on side tables, along with small white pills that he guessed were ecstasy. It was an orgy room.

"I may need you to identify him later in a photo or live line-up."

"Sure," she said, taking a drink. "Why don't you stay the night here, though? I think you'll have a life-altering experience." She reached over to one of the women and pinched her nipple. "My girlfriend and I could show you things you couldn't even dream of."

"Make sure to answer my call. If I have to come back down here, you're leaving in a police car."

As he turned to walk away she shouted, "Detective, life is too short to be so restrictive. I think you'll find that in your last days, you'll wish you'd joined us."

"It's not this life I'm worried about. Just make sure to answer your phone when I call."

CHAPTER 23

A noise invaded her dreams. It grated against her consciousness, and she tried to shrug it off. She saw herself on a beach with her mother and brother. Her father was on the porch of the old house with the dilapidated roof. Sand crabs crawled in their funny sideways walk before her bare feet, her brother squealing as he threw stones at the crabs, and her mother asking him to stop as they were God's creatures.

The sunshine was so bright that her mother forced Monique to wear sunglasses and a ridiculous amount of sunblock. Her brother was several years older and wasn't made to use as much, but he always got burnt. Her parents never seemed to mind.

Her father was trying to say something to her. She turned to him and tried to hear, but the surf was too loud. He stood in his shorts and striped shirt, smoking his pipe, and he held it up in an expressive gesture as he yelled to her, but she still couldn't hear him. The surf grew louder and louder, hurting her ears, and she put her hands up to them and screamed.

Monique bolted up in bed. The light of a dying sun came through the open window, and she could hear children playing outside. Her shirt clung to her with sweat, but the cool breeze coming through the window calmed her. She stared at the dust that swirled in the beams of light that she watched slowly begin to fade.

She heard a sound and turned to see the man sitting on a chair in the corner. He was eating out of a carton with one hand and playing with an hourglass with his other. He was completely engrossed and didn't notice that she had woken. When he saw her, he lifted another carton from the floor along with a bottle of Gatorade and put them next to her on the bed before sitting back down and continuing his play.

Monique lifted the top of the carton. She had refused food the past two days, but she couldn't refuse anymore. Her stomach ached, and her tongue felt swollen and dry from lack of moisture. She took a long drink from the bottle and then dug into the food in the carton: a gyro and French fries with a side salad.

"It's good to see you eating," he said without looking at her.

She shoved several fries into her mouth. She ate quietly and swigged half the bottle of Gatorade in one gulp.

"You should slow down. You'll get a tummy ache."

He looked at her. His face… It would've been handsome except for the burn scars and the unsettling smile that never left him.

"You haven't killed me," she said. "You haven't raped me. What *are* you gonna do with me?"

"I could do those things. Our relationship is still young."

"Do you want to kill me?"

He shrugged. "That, my young girl, was the right question. Another girl would've asked if I was going to kill her. But you asked about my desire. As a reward, I'll answer you and answer you honestly; no, I don't *want* to kill you."

"Then why are you here?"

"Why do you think? And be honest because if you lie I can tell."

She bit into her gyro and wiped her hands on her jeans. "I think you need a place to stay. If there was an old man in this house instead of me, I think he'd be tied up here."

He curled his lower lip and nodded. "Not entirely false, but not entirely true either."

"Then why did you choose here, of all places?"

"I saw you. At the bookstore."

Monique quickly scanned her memory of the last bookstore she'd been in. A Barnes & Noble near Carmel Mountain Road. Had she seen him anywhere? She'd sat in the café perusing a few books and then made a purchase. She didn't remember him there. Would she have remembered seeing someone like him?

"I didn't let you see me," he said, seemingly reading her thoughts.

"Why did you choose me?"

He spun the hourglass on the side table and stood up. "The book you were reading. Dostoevsky. It's my favorite book." He leaned down and kissed her forehead. She felt her entire body convulse in fear and disgust. "I'll be back before morning."

"Where are you going?"

"To paint the town red. Don't wait up."

CHAPTER 24

Stanton finished his afternoon surfing early and then headed inside for a quick shave and shower. By the time he'd chosen what to wear and finished his hair, it was already six in the evening. He headed out the door and saw his neighbor trying to unlock her door while holding a bag of groceries. He went and held the bag for her.

"Thanks, Jon."

"It's okay. How's your cat?"

"Vet said it was just a fever. He's doing okay now. Thanks for asking. Um, do you want to come in for some juice or something?"

"Thanks, no, I've actually got a date."

"Really? Who's the lucky gal that got you out of your apartment for once?"

"You wouldn't know her."

"Well, stop by and tell me all about it if it's not too late."

"I'll try. I better go."

"I'm not kidding, Jon, you come tell me everything that happens.

I've got female intuition."

The freeway was at a near standstill because of another accident, but as the sun was going down it painted the sky in vivid gold. Stanton turned his radio off and watched the sunset for as long as he could. Once he got past the accident, he sped down to Roosevelt and got off near the Pacific Coast Highway. There was a restaurant there right on the beach in between Los Angeles and San Diego. It was a little-known spot, mostly populated by locals. They didn't advertise, and you couldn't find them online. The only way to know about them was through word of mouth. It gave it an air of exclusivity and only added to its draw.

Stanton had discovered it with Melissa, his ex-wife. They had been surfing all day in Malibu and were starving on the drive back and needed to stop somewhere. Mel pointed to the oddly spiral-roofed building and said they should stop there.

The memory of it seared him, and he wished he'd made a reservation somewhere else.

He walked into the restaurant and saw Emma waiting for him near the hostess, chatting with her about an odd ring she had on her finger. Stanton came up behind her and waited politely until she was finished speaking.

"Oh, hey," Emma said, feeling his presence behind her.

"Hey. You didn't wait long, I hope."

"No, not at all. You ready to sit? I'm starving."

"Sure."

The hostess led them to a table next to one of the massive windows overlooking the sea. The lighting from the restaurant lit up the beach enough that he could see the waves lap the shore in thick white foam.

"I've never heard of this place," she said as a waiter brought water glasses.

"It's kinda hidden away. The owner's a real estate investor or developer or something. He doesn't need the income from this place, so he told me once he can afford to keep it pure. It's strictly a place that people are referred to by other people. No advertising at all."

"How'd you hear about it?"

"I was driving by once and stopped here."

"With your ex?"

"That obvious?"

"You cringed a little when you thought about it. How long you been divorced?"

"Going on four years now."

"Does it get easier?"

"I guess so. I miss my kids a lot. They have a stepfather now, and I think they're forgetting about me."

"They're young, I'm guessing. Young kids do that. When they get older they'll change. There's something about blood that just has a draw. People's fathers could be the worst sons of bitches on the planet, but to their kids they're still larger than life. That's just how it is, I think."

"They're good kids. I figure if I leave them alone and don't push it too hard, they'll come around. What about you? Any kids?"

"Oh, no. I've never even really been in a serious relationship. Well, once in college I dated a guy, a football player, for, like, three months, but he turned out to be an asshole. He thought it was cool to date a virgin nerd and see if he could be the first."

"Was he?"

"Of course not. He kept trying to get me drunk, and I figured out what he was doing. So I broke it off with him. Just haven't found anyone interesting since. Until I met you," she said, blushing slightly.

"Why would you say that? I'm actually pretty boring."

"No, I don't think so. There's something about you. Something kinda dark. Maybe dark's not the right word. Mysterious, enigmatic. I don't know what it is, but it forced me to say yes when you asked me out."

"Well, Professor, I think you're going to be sorely disappointed. Other than surfing, I sit home and watch reruns of *Star Trek.*"

"Oh my crap. I love *Star Trek.*"

"Really? Well, I have the DVD collection as well as a rare director's cut from one of the episodes in the second season. It's really hard to get."

"Do you think—"

The waiter interrupted and asked if they were ready to order. Stanton knew what he wanted and ordered, and Emma had to take a moment before deciding on the lobster with clam chowder as an appetizer. When the waiter had left, she took a sip of her water and excused herself to the bathroom.

Stanton looked out the windows at the ocean and saw a couple walking by, holding hands. They were barefoot and kicking sand up with each step. He turned away and checked his cell phone. There was a text from Gunn:

Did you see the report from Benny about the Brichard house???

Stanton opened his email in another window. The PDF had been attached to an email sent from one of the administrative assistants to Robbery-Homicide. He opened the PDF. After reading the first paragraph, he closed the email and called Benny.

"This is Benny."

"What do you mean it's not arson?"

"Who is this?"

"It's Jon Stanton, and I'm not in the mood for games. What do you mean it's not arson?"

"If you read the report you know what I mean."

"It was clearly arson. The family was bound up in the living room."

"I read your report. That wasn't a chain. We had it tested. It was pipe from the heating ducts in the ceiling. They fell when the roof collapsed on that section of the house, and when it melted it looked like chain. It wasn't. And we didn't find any remnants of rope or anything like that."

"There wouldn't be any remnants, Benny. That fire turned their bones to ash."

"There was still fragments of bones left."

"How'd it get so hot?"

"That I don't know. I traced the fire to an electrical wire behind the dishwasher in the kitchen. Fire spread to the living room and the bedrooms next. They were all in the living room when the fire cut off their escape. They probably just huddled together. That's what people sometimes do in a fire."

"There were windows in the living room. They would've jumped."

"People don't think clearly in a fire. They do things they wouldn't normally do. Who knows what they were thinking?"

"You don't have kids. You don't know what you think. He would have thrown his kids out the window, I promise you he would've."

"It's all conjecture, Detective. You got my report. You got a problem with it, hire your professor like you did last time."

Stanton was silent. "That's what this is about? Your ego? What are you, six years old? Are your feelings hurt that I consulted someone else?"

"Fuck you, Jon."

The phone clicked, and the call ended. Stanton dialed again, but it went to voicemail. He put his phone away. The way the family had been gathered in the living room was not chance. It wasn't a protective instinct to block themselves momentarily from the fire. They were forced into that position. Stanton knew it. He just *knew* it.

"Who was that?" Emma asked as she sat back down.

"Benny. That case I asked for your help on, he thinks it wasn't arson."

She didn't respond but instead took a sip of water and then waited for him to continue.

"Emma, he doesn't think it was arson."

"I heard you."

"You don't care?"

"Why would I care?"

"Because it clearly was. Someone's going to stay out there because Benny determined this was an accident."

"No system's perfect."

"You really don't care?"

"Not one bit."

"This guy probably killed an entire family. You're okay with that?"

"Of course I'm not okay with that, but I'm also not a superhero."

"Help me on this, Emma. There's no way this was an accident."

She shook her head. "I told you, I don't work for law enforcement. That was one time because an innocent kid was going to get railroaded."

"What about this family? They don't deserve your work because a cop happens to be investigating their case?"

"You're making me uncomfortable, Jon. I don't want to talk about this anymore."

"Well, too bad," Stanton said loudly. "A family gets burned to death, and you're going to play politics with me?"

She folded her napkin and replaced it on the table before rising. "Call me when you've calmed down."

She left, leaving Stanton sitting there, staring at her as she walked out. The waiter came over and asked if he needed anything. He said no and stood, put some cash down, went to his car, and sat in the parking lot. He thought about chasing her down, but it wouldn't do any good. He was thrown off kilter, as if someone had replaced his guts with lead weights and they bogged him down. He felt confused and angry and knew he wasn't in any shape to speak to anybody.

Stanton sat in his car and watched until her car pulled away from the curb. Then he started his car and headed home.

CHAPTER 25

Someone was pounding on Stanton's door, and he grabbed his firearm and sat up in bed. The pounding stopped for ten or twenty seconds and then started again. Stanton rose and went to the door. He looked through the peephole and saw Gunn standing with a pizza in his hand. Stanton opened the door, putting his gun on a side table.

"What are you doing here? It's like midnight."

"Not yet it's not. You eaten?"

"Yes."

Gunn pushed his way in, dropping the pizza box on the kitchen table. "Have a slice with me anyway. I haven't had dinner."

Stanton got out a plate and two cans of soda and sat down across from Gunn as he furiously shoved a molten-hot slice of pizza in his mouth. It burned his tongue, and he swore and popped open the soda, gulping half of it.

"My fucking bowels," Gunn said. "I told you this stakeout shit messes with me."

"How long were you there?"

"Since this morning." Gunn took out his phone and pulled up a document. "Guy's name is Henry Wenchowski. Polish, immigrated here 'bout thirty years ago. Married sixteen years ago, two kids. Not so much as a fucking parking ticket on his record."

"You wouldn't have come over here if you didn't have anything," Stanton said.

"You know me well."

"What'd you find?"

"Got hold of his credit card statement. Had to sift through the prick's garbage. See, he came out, like, two hours before the rest of the family was even up and threw away a little plastic sack so I checked it out. It was full of condom wrappers, cigarette packages, beer cans, and this receipt."

He pulled it out of his pocket and put it on the table. Stanton picked it up and put it next to the pizza box. It was to the Playland bar.

"He's our fucking guy," Gunn said with a mouthful of pizza.

"Who do you have on him now?"

"What d'ya mean who do I have on him? No one, it was just me."

"You left him alone on a Saturday night?"

Gunn chewed his pizza and shrugged. "Yeah, so?"

"Stephen, he's a predator. These guys are on cycles. If his cycle's up, and he's out hunting…"

"Now? No way. What are the odds of that happening?"

"We need to go to the house and arrest him now."

"With a fucking receipt?"

"I can get an ID from the manager, too. That'll give us enough for a warrant. Guys like him will always have little trophies in their house. One of Cisneros's rings or some photos."

Gunn finished his soda, wiped his hands with a napkin, and let out a large belch. "If you say so. It's your call, but if we blow our wad too early and he walks, you're gettin' the shit from Childs, not me."

They were out the door in less than five minutes and took Gunn's car, as it was parked illegally at the curb. The night air was cool, and Stanton rolled down his window and stared at the lights passing by outside. They were in the heart of the city now, the part that few outsiders ever saw—men on some corners and scantily dressed women on others. Many of the women were nearly nude. Some of them had on little more than lingerie. At a stoplight, one of the girls approached the car from the passenger side.

"You lookin' for a party, baby?"

Stanton held up his badge. The girl glanced around, as if confused, and then went back to the corner.

"Why you gotta do that?" Gunn said as the light turned, and he raced through it.

"Do what?"

"They're just working girls. Why you gotta scare the shit outta them like that? Just say no thank you and move on."

"It's easier just to show the badge."

"You never worked Vice. See, I worked Vice a long time. Most of them girls are victims. They got some pimp somewhere beating their asses every night, rapin' 'em, threatening their kids. They got hard enough lives without us bein' assholes too."

"I think that's the only time I've ever heard you actually have compassion. I'm impressed."

"Don't get all sissy on me, just be nicer to the street girls."

Their suspect's home was dark and quiet except for one light upstairs. Gunn parked the car at the curb on the opposite side of the street. Stanton kept his eyes on the lighted room. The blinds had been left open. He could see a young girl getting dressed and her mother brushing her hair.

"She's a little young to be up this late," Stanton said.

"Every family's different. My folks didn't give a shit when I went to bed."

Just then a man in a button-up plaid shirt and slacks came into the girl's room. He spoke to the mother a long while and then tucked the girl into bed and kissed her goodnight. The adults left the room together and turned off the lights.

"All's good here," Gunn said. "Can we go now?"

"Henry had his hair done. Let's wait a minute."

Gunn sighed but didn't speak. He shuffled through papers and magazines in the backseat and came up with a *Sports Illustrated*. He read by the light of the streetlamps while Stanton kept his eyes on the house. A few lights went on and off minutes later. He saw the wife, in a bathrobe, go into a bathroom. The man opened the front door and said a few things before going back to grab something in the kitchen. He disappeared around a corner.

"You ever smoked weed, Jon? I mean as, like, a kid, 'cause I know you got the Bible up your ass right now."

"No."

"I think you would really like weed. It would mellow you out. Hey, so I'm going skydivin' tomorrow. You in?"

"I've never been."

"What better time to go? I know you love surfin', but wait till you get up in the air. I got my instructor's certificate, so you can just tandem with me. Come on, I'm not takin' no for an answer."

"Do we have to spend money?"

"What the fuck kinda question is that? Why do you have to be so weird all the time?"

"It's the Sabbath. I'm not spending money on the Sabbath."

"Holy shit. All right, Jon Stanton, I swear to you that you will not have to spend any money tomorrow on a Sunday. May I be kicked in the balls by a horse if I'm lying."

"You're a true gentleman. Hey, there he is."

Henry's garage opened, and his car started, the deep red brake lights illuminating the dark. The Subaru pulled onto the street. Stanton instinctively ducked down as Gunn did the same, bringing the magazine over his face as if that would help.

Gunn sat up and started the engine, turning the car around. Stanton could see the Subaru up ahead. It came to a complete stop at an intersection then turned right. Gunn sped up and kept close, running lights and stop signs to keep up.

The Subaru stopped at a gas station, and Gunn parked across the street. Henry leaned against the door of his car as he filled his tank with gas.

"Weird lookin' dude," Gunn said.

"Why?"

"I don't know, just looks weird."

"You're just sayin' that now 'cause of what you know. Otherwise you wouldn't notice him if you walked past him."

"He doesn't look gay."

"What does someone gay look like?"

"I don't know. Skinny, dressed well, not fat. This guy looks like a fucking lumberjack."

Henry got back into his car and continued. Gunn followed. Stanton kept his eyes glued to the car, trying to see if Henry was glancing into his rearview or side mirrors. It was too dark, and they had put a lot of distance between them. It was impossible to see.

"So what'd your girlfriend think of Benny's report?"

"She won't look at it."

"Why not?"

"I honestly don't know. I don't think she likes cops."

"Oh, good. I'm sure you guys will be happy together."

"What about you? I heard you were—Stephen."

"I see it."

Henry had gunned it through a red light, forcing them to blare their horn when they went through. A truck had to slam on its brakes and swerve to avoid a collision. Gunn went into the oncoming lane and traffic scattered like insects at his approach. He tapped his brakes, twisted into the right lane, and floored the accelerator.

"What the fuck!" Gunn shouted.

"He made us. Don't lose him."

"I won't."

The Subaru sped through a stop sign and angled right, just barely missing a couple who were crossing the street. The tires screeched, and it looked about to tip, but the brake lights never came on.

Gunn made the same turn and went up on the sidewalk to avoid the couple still in the street. Several people had to jump out of his way before he could get the car back onto the road. The Subaru was still racing ahead. It ran another red light and caused a collision between two sedans. Gunn swerved around them.

"He's heading to the freeway," Stanton said. He called dispatch, giving the make and model of the Subaru and the direction they were heading. He asked for a chopper, but dispatch told him that both choppers were occupied and they'd get one there as fast as possible.

The on-ramp was clear, and the Subaru sped up and quickly merged, getting over two lanes before Gunn had even made it past the on-ramp.

"Get to the left lane," Stanton said.

A semi came up beside them, and every time Gunn tried to get over, the semi sped up. Gunn blared his horn and flipped him off. The driver kept speeding up, so Gunn took out his firearm and held it out the window. The semi immediately slowed down, and Gunn got over two lanes.

The freeway was busy but not congested. The Subaru was maybe sixty feet ahead, darting in and out of oncoming traffic. From the far left lane it suddenly twisted violently to the right as it tried to maneuver into another lane. It spun all the way around before crossing three lanes of traffic and crashing into a barrier.

"We got him," Gunn said.

The door opened, and Henry struggled out, blood leaking from a cut on his forehead. He stumbled into traffic and nearly got clipped by a mini-van before jumping the railing and half-falling down a slope.

Gunn hit his brakes in front of the Subaru, and the two men leapt out and started running. Gunn was over the railing without looking, and Stanton took a moment to catch sight of Henry, who was racing down the hill. Stanton hopped the railing and followed them. Gunn was yelling, "Police!" but Henry wasn't slowing down.

A hundred feet away stood some abandoned factories and warehouses that had gone bust years ago when the real estate market bottomed out. Now they sat vacant, too expensive to rent and too much of a hassle to buy.

The first building was six stories. It was rusted and broken down, with graffiti and boarded-up windows. Henry swung open the door and ran inside, Gunn right after him. Stanton pulled out his Desert Eagle and followed.

The interior smelled like burnt oil and dust. Henry's and Gunn's footfalls were so loud that it felt as if they shook the building. It was too dark to see where they were; the only light was the moon coming in through the broken windows, but Stanton could hear them a floor above him now. He took out a penlight and saw stairs at the far side.

The stairs shook as he took them two at a time. He saw Henry running up another set of stairs to the next floor. Gunn was right behind him, no more than twenty feet. Stanton sprinted for them. By the time he got to the next set of stairs, they were already heading to the next floor. But he could hear the wheezing and the swearing—Henry was tiring.

"I got you, motherfucker!" Gunn bellowed through the warehouse. A loud crash was followed by a scream.

Stanton raced to the other set of stairs and to the next floor. He put his penlight in his teeth and went gun first along the railing. He saw a mass of movement in front of him. Henry was on his back as Gunn punched him in the face.

"That's enough," Stanton said. "We got him."

Gunn struck him several more times and then stood up, rubbing his right fist, which was now covered in blood. "Bastard bit me."

Stanton shone his light on Gunn's hand. There were indentations of teeth, but they didn't break the skin. "You'll be okay."

Before Stanton could stop him, Gunn kicked Henry so hard he twisted to his side and vomited. Stanton grabbed Gunn, pinning him against the railing.

"That's enough. He's down," Stanton said.

"Motherfucker," Gunn said, out of breath, his eyes pinned on the man writhing on the floor. "You cuff him and get his ass to the car. If I do it, he ain't gonna make it the whole way."

CHAPTER 26

Nehor Stark went around the small house and made sure the clear liquid had doused the frame. The windows were soaked, as were the doors. The interior was covered, and the vapors were only a soft hint seeping out of the house and tingling his nose.

Only one more place to wet before the show.

He ran around the perimeter of the house. It was red brick with white trim and had a nice fence surrounding it. The neighborhood was upscale, and he had to hide in the bushes when a group of teenagers peeled out of their parents' driveway across the street in a new Mercedes. The car came back for some reason, and one of the girls ran back inside. He watched her legs, silky and smooth underneath the lamplight. As she came back out, she glanced up, and their eyes locked.

Nehor immediately turned to his right and looked down at the sidewalk, pretending to be passing through. He dropped the fuel canister into some bushes and walked for a few moments before looking back at the taillights of the Mercedes up the street. He ran back to the house and put on his backpack.

There was a shed in the back that held the lawnmower and other equipment. He sprinted for it and jumped, swinging his legs onto the roof and standing up. He glanced around to see if anyone had seen, but the neighborhood was empty. He climbed onto the roof of the house.

The sky was dark with the exception of two stars and the moon, gray-black clouds slowly drifting by and covering the light until the icy glow returned a few moments later. Nehor watched the moon a long time and then removed his backpack and undressed. The blood spatter on his clothes looked black in the moonlight. He thought it oddly beautiful that it appeared darker than anything he had ever seen.

Nude, he opened the backpack and lifted the small canister of fuel. He began dousing the roof, going in geometric shapes: circles first and then a pentagram. The pentagram would show through the fire; it didn't mean anything to him, but the neighbors would be unsettled every time they looked over at the house. Maybe some of them would even have to move out.

When the canister was empty, he threw his clothes and backpack on the front lawn and climbed down using the shed in the backyard. He went to the front of the house and stood on the lawn, listening to his breathing. He reached down into his duffel bag, brought out the matchbox, and opened it to remove the match. He held it lightly in his fingers and twisted it to the left and the right. He quivered and was sweating visibly. It glistened in the moonlight.

He struck the match.

The front door was open, and he flung the match on the porch. The porch instantly burst into three-foot-high flames, which raced around like a caged animal trying to find a way to escape. They dashed inside the house, and the flames grew. Within thirty seconds, smoke billowed out in large clouds, darker than the night, and he could hear the screaming coming from inside. The flames flourished, and the roof caught fire; there was, in a single instant, a powerful, thunderous, glorious explosion. There was barely any house left standing as the fire engulfed it.

Nehor stepped close to the inferno. He was erect now. He wanted to inhale the wondrous smoke, but he wouldn't last longer than a minute before he lost consciousness. One day, when he found somewhere secluded enough, he would indulge himself. But for now he approached the flames cautiously.

The fire was so hot it melted the barbeque on the front porch and singed his skin, and he felt his pubic hair catch fire, the tips lit red as they coiled like burning ants. He made a note to shave himself next time.

His skin was boiling. He could feel the heat inside him as sweat drained from every pore. It was cleansing him. He felt himself burning away, his memories, his thoughts, his emotions… They were lifted into the night like ashes and drifted away. The only things he could feel now were the pain and the heat that made him feel faint.

Another explosion flung him onto his back. The screaming had stopped; the fire had eaten that. He looked back and saw one of the neighbors on his porch, phone to his ear. Nehor grabbed his clothes and the bag and ran to the car that waited for him up the street.

Monique Gaspirini woke to the sound of her car pulling into the garage. She was huddled underneath the sheets. They were pulled over her head and covered every inch of her. It was something she used to do as a child to protect herself from the boogeyman, and she had found these past few days that she couldn't sleep unless the sheets were over her head.

As the door opened downstairs, she thought of her mother and why she hadn't called. Then again, she never called. They didn't check up on her, and Monique had always thought she liked it that way, but she would have given anything to hear her mother's voice on the other end of the phone.

Footfalls on the stairs. They were fast, faster than usual. Monique heard the door to her room open, but she didn't want to take the sheets off. She didn't want to see him. As long as she didn't see him, she could pretend he wasn't real.

The light turned on. She smelled an odor from him she hadn't smelled before—like burnt rubber. Slowly, she slid the sheets off her head and looked.

He stood in the doorway, nude and fully erect. Smoke was coming off his skin in barely visible wafts, and all the hair on his body had been singed. The skin on his belly appeared to be peeling. She saw his look, the horrible look as he stared down at her.

She screamed.

CHAPTER 27

Stanton watched Henry Wenchowski through the two-way mirror. He was nervous and fidgeting with a ring on his finger—his wedding ring. He looked like a kind uncle or perhaps a young grandfather.

Gunn stood over him, questioning him. Henry denied everything and insisted he had witnesses to prove where he'd been the night of the murder. He appeared shocked to be accused of being gay and asked for a lawyer. Stanton stepped in.

"Stephen, why don't you grab a drink and call the public defender's office? Let's see if we can find him a lawyer."

Gunn shrugged and left the room.

Stanton sat down across from Henry. "How old are your girls?"

"Twelve and ten."

"My kids are boys. I've heard girls are easier."

"They definitely take care of their father better, at least I think. I don't have any boys."

Stanton leaned back in his chair. "I'm sorry we have to do this to you, Henry. You seem like a decent guy. I wish there was another way."

"I've asked for a lawyer," he said, glancing away.

"We're getting you one, but we gotta wake up a public defender. They might not get in till morning. So like it or not, you're with us for the night. Don't worry, I'm not asking you about the case. I just wanted to let you know that I'm sorry. Will you chat with me while we wait for a lawyer?"

"Fine, but if you're truly sorry, then why don't you let me go?" he said desperately. "I'm telling you, there are at least three people who will testify to where I was that night."

"I have no doubt, and if it was only the Cisneros thing, I'd let you go. But you ran. That's a felony, running from the cops."

"I was scared. I didn't know who you two were. If I'd known you were cops I certainly wouldn't have run like that."

"I believe you. But at this point it's out of my hands." He leaned forward. "You've already asked for a lawyer so anything you tell me can't be used against you, but I'm curious about something. Will you talk to me without your lawyer if I ask you a question about something in the case?"

"What question?"

"Does your wife know you're gay?"

"I am not—"

"Henry, we're civilized men. Lying to each other doesn't become us. It's not polite."

Henry bit his lower lip and looked away. He said, quietly, almost a whisper, "No, she doesn't know."

"What would she do if she found out?"

"She'd leave me, of course. She's a good Christian woman. She wouldn't tolerate that."

"I'm sorry, Henry. I'm sorry you have to be in this situation, and I'm sorry you have to hide your true self. My uncle was gay and I saw the pain he had to go through just because he loved a little differently than other people."

"Please," he whispered, tears welling in his eyes. "Just let me go. Just let me live my life, and I swear you'll never see me again. Never."

Stanton reached out and held his hand. "All right, Henry. I'm going to trust you. I'm going to assume that you can get those witnesses to me. I want them to call me tomorrow. Can they do that?"

"Yes, of course. First thing."

"Okay, have them call me, and if they verify your story, we won't file charges."

"Oh, thank you. Thank you," he said, weeping. "You don't know what this means to me."

"I'm being honest with you, but I want you to be honest with me. Can you do that?"

"Yes."

"Were you having an affair with Michael Cisneros?"

"Yes," he said, breaking down, his head lowered.

"Did you do what you did because he was going to tell your wife? Because he was trying to destroy you?"

"Yes, yes." He wiped the tears away from his eyes. "He said he was coming to my house. He wanted me to leave my wife, and I said no. I love my wife. But he wouldn't stop. He just wouldn't stop. And then he showed up at my house. At my house!"

"What did you stab him with?"

"I don't know. Some kitchen knife. Something on hand. He wouldn't stop moving and so I... I just kept stabbing. I just wanted him to stop moving."

"Okay, okay, it's okay, Henry. You're going to be okay." Stanton rose. "Wait here for me."

"Can I go now?"

"Not yet."

Stanton walked out. Gunn and another three detectives were standing in front of the two-way, and they started clapping.

"That," Gunn said, "is how you get a fucking confession."

"What about his asking for a lawyer?" one of the younger detectives asked.

"No good," Gunn said. "Jon asked him again if he could talk to him without a lawyer, and he consented. Twice. In California, consent negates the askin'." Gunn bowed to Stanton. "The master."

Stanton left without saying anything. He had done his job. The Supreme Court of the United States had long held that police officers were allowed to lie about everything to garner a confession. But every time he did it, it took a piece of him. He didn't enjoy it in the least and felt no triumph, no joy in the act of catching a killer. But there was no choice. No one else could do it, and he wouldn't have stopped killing. Not after he saw how easy it was.

"What's the matter?" Gunn said, catching up.

"I've never enjoyed that part of it."

"You kiddin' me? That prick cuts up some young kid and you're broken up for lyin' to him?" Gunn put his arm around him. "Come on, we're goin' to a bar to celebrate."

Coochie's stank of beer and old vomit. It was a surfer bar that had been converted to a cop bar after several officers made a habit of going there after their shifts. The owners were former Highway Patrol and didn't mind the change.

Stanton, Gunn, and several uniforms sat in the corner booth, drinking and telling war stories. Stanton sipped a Diet Coke and listened. The drunker they got, the more outlandish the stories and the more heroic their behavior. One officer was telling the story of how two drug dealers—lesbians—had offered him a threesome to let them go. He said he didn't take them up on it, and the men started laughing and shoving him. He appeared to blush and didn't say anything further about it.

"What about you, Jon?" one of the uniforms said. "You ever take some cream or a bit of pussy?"

"This guy?" Gunn laughed. "This guy feels bad 'cause he lied to a piece'a shit murderer."

"Oh shit," one of the uniforms said, "you goin' pussy on us, Johnny boy?"

"Goin'?" Gunn said. "Nah, I'm just playin'. He's going skydivin' with me tomorrow, and that takes balls." Gunn downed the remnants of a whiskey. "You know what? Fuck that, let's go now."

"What?" Stanton said.

"Let's go now. I ain't kiddin'."

"In the dark?"

"Hell yes, in the dark."

"I don't think we can do that."

"I'm an instructor; we can do whatever we want."

"I'll pass, Stephen."

"I'll tell you what. You come skydivin' with me tonight, right now, and I'll tell you why your little girlfriend won't help us."

"What do you mean?"

"I mean I did some checking up. I'll tell you why she won't help us."

"Why?"

"Nope. You gotta go night-divin' with me. Right now."

The men started thumping their fists against the table chanting,

"Go, go, go, go, go!"

"Do you really know?" Stanton said. "'Cause if you don't, and I do this, I'm going to shoot you in the knees."

"Hand to heaven. I know exactly why she won't help us."

"Stephen, that's an important case. An entire family was killed. If you know something—"

"I seen kids spattered in the gutters and old men beaten to death by twelve-year-olds. You ain't tuggin' on any heartstrings, my man. You want the info, you gotta come with me."

"You'll tell me eventually."

"Nope. I'll get super drunk and probably forget what it was. I swear to you, I won't tell you."

Stanton finished his Diet Coke. "All right, let's go."

The other officers cheered as they climbed out of the booth and headed out to their cars. The airfield was a good twenty miles away, and Gunn called ahead as Stanton drove. The pilot was called in as a special favor in exchange for a case of Jack Daniels—which Gunn would get at a fifty percent discount through a source he never talked about—and the plane was fueled and ready to go.

The airfield was in the Otay Mesa community, right near the

US/Mexico border. As they drove through the neighborhood, several crowds of young men were gathered in the streets, smoking weed and drinking. The officers honked their horns and yelled out the windows at them. A few were in cruisers, and many of the men ran inside as soon as they saw them, thinking they were about to be raided.

The plane was already on the strip, and the pilot was sitting outside smoking. He threw his cigarette down and boarded when he saw them drive up.

"I really don't want to do this," Stanton said.

"You got one life, Johnny baby, you gotta enjoy it, man." Gunn slapped his chest. "You're gonna have a blast. Or you're gonna die. Either way it'll be a story to tell. Come on."

They hopped out to the shouts of the other officers who were sitting on the hoods of their cars and cheering them on. Gunn led Stanton aboard the plane and got out two packs.

"It's gonna be cold as hell, and you're gonna freeze your nuts off. Them Mormon underwear you got on, are they warm?"

"Not really."

"Well, you may wanna put on a dive suit. We got one on the plane."

"Let's just get this over with."

"You ever dive before?"

"You're drunker than I thought. I told you I've never been."

"Calm down now, booze affects the memory. So 'cause you never been, you're gonna hang onto me. Easy-peasy. You spread-eagle, don't arch, don't get your knees too far down, don't have your legs too far apart, don't have your arms too far out front. You seen the position on TV right?"

"I think so."

"Well, we got some time on the plane. Come on, we can practice."

They boarded, and the plane roared to life. It jerked forward and began to move down the strip and then slowed as it made a turn. Then, with open pavement before it, it gained speed until Stanton had to hang on to something. It jerked a couple of times and lifted into the air. The wheels groaned as they were folded underneath and they soared, higher and higher.

They went over proper positioning to prevent too much air pressure, the emergency chute location, and checking the harness. Then Gunn clipped Stanton's harness to his own, and they were literally joined at the hip. Gunn shouted that he would be holding onto him as they exited the plane and would correct his posture on the way down. When they hit the right altitude, he would initiate the chute, so Stanton didn't have to worry about that, either.

The door opened, and Stanton got a look at the drop zone beneath them—the airfield, lit up with floodlights. But it was still dark enough that he couldn't judge the proper distance for the fall. The air was screaming so loudly it drowned out Gunn's last-minute instructions, but the adrenaline was flowing so powerfully that it wouldn't have mattered anyway. The only things Stanton could hear were the wind and the pounding of his heart.

"Tell me why," Stanton shouted.

"No way, after the jump. If both of us live." Gunn looked at the pilot who gave him a thumbs-up. "You ready?"

Stanton nodded.

They stepped to the edge of the door, the night sky before them like some vast painting, the moon lighting up the water of the Pacific, and they jumped.

The power of the wind against his goggles and the icy feeling on his exposed skin woke Stanton up as he had never been awakened before. He was acutely aware of his surroundings. It didn't feel like motion; it felt as if he were floating, but the cold air making him shiver told him he was falling. Gunn kept pulling up his arms or pushing down his knees or fixing the arch in his back. But Stanton couldn't take his eyes off the Pacific and its vastness of space, black and unknown. He glanced up at the moon and felt as if he hadn't seen it before.

The one problem that nagged him was that he couldn't tell how far away the ground truly was. It was exhilarating and terrifying at once. But he kept himself calm, though his heart pounded in his ears like a drum.

When they were at a certain altitude that Stanton couldn't guess, Gunn pulled his cord, and both of them seemed to shoot up as their chute opened. It was a sudden, jerking motion, and it rattled him before the smooth descent began. Stanton could now see his surroundings in a way he couldn't during the free-fall. It was a 360-degree view of the city of San Diego and the Pacific Ocean, with glimpses into Mexico. San Diego was bright and vibrant while the Mexican side had few lights but more open fields and groves of trees that appeared black as tar in the night. But the ocean drew him, and that was where he kept his eyes. It shimmered and moved; it appeared alive.

Gunn was shouting something, but he couldn't hear what. Then he started waving his arms. Gunn cupped his hands over his mouth, and Stanton could barely make it out. He was saying, "Almost there."

Stanton braced himself, but because the ground was so dark, he couldn't anticipate when he would land. By the time he realized he was just barely off the ground, he had only enough time to bend his knees and hit the ground hard. He tumbled head over heels several times and lay flat on his back, his breathing heavy and labored, as Gunn awkwardly unbuckled and rolled next to him.

They both collapsed, and Gunn was yelling, for some reason.

"How was it?" Gunn asked. "No, don't tell me. Words just fuck things up."

They lay there for several minutes, breathing heavy, watching the stars, until Stanton said, "Why?"

"Her dad. He was executed in Texas for murder. They think now that maybe he was innocent. Guess what he was accused of?"

Stanton didn't have to guess. He knew the moment Gunn had asked: it was arson.

CHAPTER 28

Stanton lay in bed, staring at the ceiling. Though it was well past six in the morning, he couldn't sleep and had been up all night. The rush of skydiving was still with him, and he could hear the wind in his ears. His heart started pounding again for no reason, and he got butterflies in his stomach. Also his head and his back ached from the landing, and he thought he had injured his knee.

He tried to sleep, but the fatigue would only wash over him for so long before he would wake and stare at the ceiling again. He turned on some music, soft jazz, and drank a glass of warm milk.

At eight in the morning his cell phone woke him from a brief sleep. He was exhausted and thought about just turning it off, but decided to check. It might be his ex saying something was wrong with his boys.

The caller ID on his phone said, "NATHAN SELL."

"This is Stanton."

"Jon, it's Nate, man. Get your ass up, I got something for you."

"What is it?"

"Got a call about a homicide up here in Old Town. I was gonna work it when someone mentioned it was similar to something you got."

"What is it?"

"Fire."

Stanton's heart dropped. "Is it a family?"

"Yeah, man. Six kids and the mom and dad. You believe that?"

"What made them think homicide?"

"One of the uniforms used to be a lab tech and smelled the accelerant. He called it in. I got Benny comin' out in a few hours."

"I'll be right down."

Stanton wrote the address on his palm and then put it into his phone. He got dressed without showering or shaving and was out the door in less than ten minutes.

He got up to Old Town quickly. He turned on a classical station, but couldn't concentrate and turned it off.

The neighborhood was a mass of fire engines, police cruisers, neighbors, and ambulances. The ME's van was parked on the sidewalk, and an SUV with "SIS" on the side was parked behind it. Stanton came to a stop near the police tape before getting out.

Nathan Sell was tall and lean in a gray suit. He stood on the sidewalk, watching the men work the house. Homicide detectives could do little at suspected arson sites, but they had to be there, supervising the work. Someone's butt had to be on the line if something went wrong.

"You got anything?" Stanton said, coming up to him.

"Not a damn thing. The temperature got so hot most of the jewelry in the bedroom's melted. The bodies... there's not much left."

"I need to see them."

"Have at it."

Stanton ducked under the tape and continued up the driveway. Nothing was left of the house but a few pieces of the frame and a half-melted shed in the back. He found a tech's bag near what used to be the front door and got booties on his feet before going in.

The walls had been completely burned away, and he could see the remnants of the family. Eight blackened skeletons huddled together in the living room. Nothing surrounded them as the melted metal had at the prior scene; nothing indicated they had been tied together. The father—or what Stanton guessed had been the father—had his arms around the younger children, trying to protect them from the flames.

Stanton turned away and left.

"Well?" Nathan said.

"It's the same. The same person did this."

Nathan shook his head. "Some days, I wish I'd gone to business school like my mama told me to."

A van pulled up—Channel 4 News, the NBC affiliate. A leggy blonde stepped out of the passenger side, and an overweight man with a Chargers cap jumped out of the driver's side, and they met up with another man who came out of the back. They gathered some equipment, the second man held a mirror for the blonde to check her make-up, and they ducked under the police tape.

"Vultures," Nathan said, stepping toward them.

"No," Stanton said. "I want them here."

"You sure?"

"Yes, I need to talk to them."

"Your ass."

Stanton joined them. He knew the blonde. She had been to several crime scenes over the past six months and was aggressive. Many reporters tried to get in people's faces, but she went about it the right way, waiting until everyone had cleared out before hitting detectives up one-on-one with the tough questions.

"Detective Stanton," she said, a smile on her face, "you got a quote for me other than 'no comment' or 'get behind the tape'?"

"How about 'I want to give you an exclusive interview'?"

"I'd say you want something in return. Sorry, I got a boyfriend, although you are cute," she said, rubbing his chest with her fingers.

"What I want is much simpler: I want this to be breaking news on Channel 4 right now and on every broadcast today."

"I can't do that. It's the producer who makes—"

"Your name's Katherine, right?"

"Yeah."

"Katherine, we could both sit here and try to convince the other that our hands are tied on all the things we want to do and that the orders are coming down from on high, but we both know that's garbage. This is my scene, and I can do what I want with it. This is your segment, and you can do what you want. The producer won't fight you on it."

She smiled. "I always thought you were smarter than you looked. Okay, lemme make a call."

Stanton waited while she took out her cell phone and spoke in hushed tones with someone. He turned away from the scorched house and looked across the street. The home there had a bicycle in the driveway and toys on the lawn. A toddler came out with her mother, and the mother was forcing her to pick up her toys. It made Stanton smile, and he forgot for a moment what he was doing. When the mother saw all the vehicles and the smoking ruins of her neighbor's house, she grabbed her child and went back inside.

"All right, Detective," Katherine said. "You got a deal."

"Okay, you ready?"

"One sec."

They checked her makeup again and then sound and visual. When the cameraman was ready, the assistant who had checked her makeup moved behind him and watched. There was an earpiece in Katherine's ear now, hardly more than a clear bit of plastic, and she was nodding along to a conversation somewhere else as if everyone could hear it.

"That's right, Christopher, I'm here at the scene right now with Detective Jonathan Stanton of the San Diego Police Department's Homicide Unit, and we're looking at what was once a beautiful two-story home on La Brea Drive. As you can see, it's just ashes now." She turned to Stanton. "Now, Detective, it's early in the case, but the fact that the Homicide Unit has sent someone—I think we can safely assume that the police department believes this to be a homicide."

"We do, yes."

"And is there any evidence of that here?"

"Well, I can't speak too much about an ongoing investigation, but what I can tell you is that the pattern of the homicide is nearly identical to another fire we had last week, and that also is still under investigation. The victims were nearly identical—a family of four there. The only difference here is that there were eight lives taken, six of them children. One was a baby of probably no more than eighteen months."

"It's hard to imagine who would do something like this to children."

"Well, monsters exist. They're out there, and they're hunting. This monster is particularly dangerous because he targets families and takes out a large number of victims at once."

"I know you stated you can't talk about the details of an ongoing investigation, but are there any leads you're exploring right now that could lead to a suspect? Any help that our viewers may be able to give?"

"Unfortunately, no. The evidence in this case has burned away with the rest of the house. As of this moment, we have no leads. The sad fact is, Katherine, that we may not be able to capture him before he commits another one of these crimes. So I'm asking anyone out there, if they have any information that could help us find who did this, please call the tip hotline on the website for San Diego PD. You could be saving many lives."

"Thank you, Detective, for your time here, and good luck."

"Thank you."

Stanton waited until she had finished the segment and the camera was turned off. "I'm going to have one of my officers track down a photo of the family for you. Can you show it on the segment?"

"Sure. Out of curiosity, why are you so anxious to help?"

"There's someone who I need to see this segment. Thanks for this. I appreciate it."

"Anytime. I think I should say you owe me one."

"You got it."

Nathan whistled through his teeth. "You are going to get your ass reamed for that, my man. You made us look like we have our heads up our asses and this guy is outsmarting us. Childs's head is going to explode."

"I know, but I had to do it."

"If you say so." He turned back to the house. "You got this?"

"Yeah, I'll be here if anyone asks."

Stanton joined the techs and uniforms as they waited for Benny to arrive. They did a walk-through of the house and then began canvasing the neighborhood.

Several of the neighbors said they heard nothing until there was an explosion. Many of them thought it was an earthquake at first, and they were panicking until they got outside and saw the flames consuming the house. Stanton knocked on one door across the street and an old man in a bathrobe answered.

"SDPD, we're investigating the fire across the street."

"What fire?"

Stanton stepped to the side so he could see. The man squinted, mumbled something about getting his glasses and then went back inside for a moment. When he returned with his bifocals on, he studied the house but was still squinting.

"I'll be damned. I thought I smelled smoke, but I gotta take so many of them damn sleeping pills I thought I was having a dream." The man looked at Stanton, as if he'd just noticed him for the first time. "Don't think I can help you, Officer."

"Thanks anyway."

The next house was much larger and better kept. Stanton knocked on the door, and a middle-aged woman in workout clothes answered. He asked her if she had seen anything, and she said that they had all been asleep.

As the woman was speaking, Stanton noticed the girl sitting on the stairs listening. She was fifteen or sixteen and seemed intensely interested in what was being said. The woman mentioned hearing a car a short time before the fire.

"How long before?"

"I couldn't say. I didn't see the fire start, but the explosion did wake us up. It was, I dunno, maybe fifteen or twenty minutes before that. Around five in the morning."

"What's your daughter's name?"

"Tabitha. Why?"

"May I speak to her?"

"I guess, but I told you she doesn't know anything, Detective."

"If I can just have a word." Stanton saw the hesitation on the woman's face. "Sometimes teenagers can hear things others can't. They have more sensitive hearing because of their age and hormones."

"Whatever you say." She turned to the girl and said, "Come talk to the detective."

The girl sighed and came over. She rolled her eyes, folded her arms, and leaned against the doorframe.

"Hi, Tabitha. My name is Jon, and I'm with the San Diego Police Department. I'm trying to figure out what happened last night, and I just wanted to know if you saw or heard anything."

"No. Mom already told you we were asleep."

"So you were in your bed asleep around five in the morning?"

"Yes."

"Do you share the room with anyone?"

"No, it's just mine."

Stanton ran his tongue across the back of his teeth as he considered her. She had glanced to the left when she said she was in her room. Leftward glancing during conversation tended to indicate constructed images or sounds, whereas glancing right tended to indicate remembered images or sounds, correlating to the logic and creative hemispheres of the brain. She had also used distancing language: instead of "my mom" it was just "mom." Instead of "my room" she had said "it's." She was physically distancing herself from Stanton, as well, by folding her arms; people who were lying typically only moved limbs toward their bodies.

With her mother standing right behind her, though, there was no way she would reveal anything.

"Okay, Tabitha, thanks. If you think of anything, you'll let me know, right?"

"Sure," she said, turning away and heading up the stairs.

Stanton turned toward the burned house and saw Benny arrive. There was another arson investigator that the police department liked to use, but Stanton couldn't remember his name. He would have to look that up when he got back to the precinct.

His phone rang. There were two calls he was waiting for, and this one had come much more quickly than he would've thought.

"Hi, Danny."

"You out of that damn multiple-wife-havin', magic-underwear-wearin' mind of yours? What the fuck did you go on the news for?"

"I had to—"

"No, no, fuck you. Fuck you, Jon. I had to sit at my desk and have Chin Ho chew my ass for ten minutes. Do you know what kinda panic this'll cause? How many old farts with itchy trigger fingers will blow their neighbors' heads off 'cause they think it's a damn arsonist?"

"I know, but I had to risk—"

"Get your ass back here right now."

"I'm working the scene."

"Fuck the scene. Get back here, now!"

The phone clicked. Stanton took a deep breath as he walked to his car and watched Benny get his kit out of the truck and go to work.

CHAPTER 29

Stanton sat in a chair in front of Lieutenant Daniel Childs's desk. Captain Phillips was away, and Chin Ho had delegated the task of yelling at him to Childs. Stanton watched as Childs folded his arms in front of him on the desk, his muscles bulging underneath the tight long-sleeved shirt he had on.

"You're off this case."

"I know what I did was risky. But the only way I could get the help we need was to run a segment like that."

"You had one of the uniforms give a photo of the family to the news. Them kids' grandparents called us. We hadn't had a chance to notify next of kin yet. That's how they found out all six of their grandkids was dead."

"I'm sorry, but it wouldn't have been any easier coming from you."

"What did you say?"

"This isn't an accident. This is a *pattern*. We have something unique here, something we haven't dealt with before. Benny is useless on this case. I need Emma to help."

"Who the fuck is Emma? That professor you brought in on the last one? Well, you ain't got to worry about it 'cause I'm giving this case to Nate and Slim Jim. Now get outta my office."

"Danny, you and I go back a long ways, you know me. Do you really think I'm wrong about this?"

Childs shook his head. "That's your problem, man. That's why I'm sitting in this chair and you're sittin' in that one even though you're ten times the detective I was. It don't matter if you're wrong or right. You gotta do things the way the higher-ups want. You think I don't know they fuck up your cases? You think I don't know dope dealers go free every damned day 'cause we gotta get approval to spend sixty dollars for flash money to make a fake buy? You think I don't see the captain's friends getting let off of DUIs and bar fights just 'cause they know him? Don't forget I been a cop longer than you. I know it all, man. And I'm telling you, it don't matter."

Stanton rose. "It does matter. And if you don't do anything about it, you're no better than them."

Stanton drove away from the precinct well over the speed limit. He didn't feel like working any cases or speaking to any victims right now. He felt like getting his board and heading out into the ocean and being alone on the waves, if they would have him. But his cell phone rang incessantly and interrupted his thoughts. He answered, and it was his ex asking for changes to child support payments this month, then his psychiatrist's office called to confirm his appointment for tomorrow, and then Gunn called.

"Hey, man. I just heard we're off the arson cases."

"Yeah, well, what can you do?"

"Oh, man. Why is it I get scared when you act defeated?"

"What?"

"You're not stoppin' on these cases, are you?"

"They're heading in the wrong direction. And who's going to work them? Benny? We used to have a Metro Arson Strike Team, and now we have *Benny?*"

"Metro Arson cost us an arm and a leg, my friend. You like makin' more than someone at McDonald's? Then I suggest you don't complain. Now look, get this shit outta your head. I ain't gettin' suspended 'cause of a couple of fires. Besides, we got somethin' more interestin' on our plates."

"What is it?"

"Western called over and asked for some help on a scene. They thought it was a massacre, but it turned out it was just one vic, a young woman. I'm headed down there right now. You should come, too. The news is already there. Supposed to be some fucked up shit."

"I appreciate you trying to cheer me up with… that, but I think I'm heading out to surf."

"All right, look, they asked me for help, but this sounds like one sick fuck. I need your help."

"What do you care about a case out of Western? It's not our jurisdiction. Let them handle it."

"Oh, shit. Look who cares about proper procedure and jurisdiction now? It's my fuckin' ex-wife's case, okay."

"I thought you weren't speaking."

"I thought so too, but she called and said I may be able to help her. Can you come?"

Stanton sighed. "Yeah, sure, just text me the address. I'm on my way."

An hour and thirty-five minutes of sitting in traffic later, Stanton pulled up to Maplewood Drive. Crowds had gathered behind the police tape. He watched their faces, their reactions. Some had brought out lawn chairs.

Several police cruisers and an SIS/CSI van were parked nearby. Stanton walked to the tape and showed his badge to a uniform he didn't recognize. The man was large, muscular beyond comfort, and asked him a few questions about what he was doing here rather than just letting him through, which was more customary. Stanton politely answered the questions and heard someone call his name behind him. Gunn ran up and went to duck under the police tape when the uniform stopped him.

"What are you here for?"

"What? Fuck you, dickhead. Get the fuck outta my way and go write some traffic tickets." Gunn brushed past him, and Stanton followed. "You see Erin yet?"

"No, I just got here."

The house was large, three stories with a yard. There was a car parked in the driveway, and the driver's side door was open. They made their way up past the car and glanced in before going inside the house.

Music, a classic rock station, was playing somewhere. Gunn's ex-wife Erin Dallas was standing by a pattern of blood spatter on the wall, directing the forensic techs. Another tech was walking around the house with a camera filming the scene, and there were a couple of other detectives, as well. A newspaper reporter sat on the couch with a laptop, his press badge dangling from his lanyard.

"How you doin', baby?" Gunn said.

"Steve, I'm glad you came. Hello, Jon."

"It's good to see you, Erin."

"You too." She turned to Gunn. "So you want the quick rundown or you guys wanna explore for a bit? Don't mind the music; it was playing when we got here."

"Just tell me what you got."

"One victim, twenty-three, Monique Gaspirini. She's, well, what's left of her is upstairs in the bedroom. Let's head up there."

They followed her through the house, forensics giving them booties and latex gloves to put on. There were masks, as well, and while everyone coming down the stairs wore them, Gunn and Stanton declined.

As they passed the kitchen, Stanton looked over and saw one of the techs taking photos of a frying pan on the burner. He stopped and looked more closely at what was in the pan: a human heart. Part of a heart, anyway, and Stanton noticed the other portion on a plate on a dining room table in the adjacent room.

"You fuckin' kiddin' me?" Gunn said when he saw what Stanton was looking at.

"It gets worse," Erin said.

They climbed the stairs and saw stains on the carpets, boot prints outlined in blood. At the top of the stairs, they turned left toward a bedroom, and Erin opened the half-closed door.

The room looked like the back of a butcher's shop. Blood, hair, organs and tissue were smeared on the walls. Something was nailed on the closet door; it appeared to be a kidney. On the bed were the remains of what Stanton guessed was once a human being.

"If you notice," Erin said, pointing with a pen she held in her hand, "the face is missing. We haven't found it yet but he—or they— might've taken it as a trophy."

"It's one man," Stanton said softly.

"How do you know?"

"There's only one set of boot prints going down the stairs." He leaned down, closer to the bed. Though her legs were still there, they had been severed from her torso.

"You ever seen anythin' like this?" Gunn mumbled.

"No," Stanton said, rising.

Gunn turned to Erin. "Why did you call us out here, Er? You got enough manpower without us buttin' in."

"I've never… I don't think I'm the best qualified for this type of case. I'm happy to do it, and I can figure it out as I go, but I could use a head start. If I went to other detectives in my precinct, well, it's hard enough being one of only three females in Homicide. I don't need to go begging for help, too. They'd lose respect for me. But I also know what I don't know. And I don't know what this is."

Stanton swallowed and turned to the only window in the room. He walked over to it and looked down onto the street. A tech walked in and began filming and taking measurements.

"All right," Gunn said, "we'll help you. What d'ya need?"

"Just what I said, a head start. We've notified the family and are talking to all the neighbors, but it doesn't sound like anybody has anything to say other than that they're shocked."

"She have a boyfriend?" Stanton asked.

"Yes, but we haven't been able to get hold of him. One of the neighbors said she'd seen a man here a few days ago, but it could be her boyfriend. She's working with a sketch artist right now to get us a face."

Stanton turned toward the girl. He noticed something on her right shoulder. He bent down over her. His heart was racing. He was always afraid the dead weren't truly dead, and hardly anything would have frightened him more than to have one of them sucking in breath, crying for help when there was nothing he could do.

"Look at this," Stanton said. The other two crowded around and looked where he was pointing, at a small circular wound on the flesh.

"Cigarette?" Gunn said.

"No, but it's definitely something involving heat. The outer dermis is completely melted away."

"Huh," Erin said.

The tech behind them said, "I need photos of her back if you guys want to help me lift."

Erin nodded, and they gently lifted the girl up as the tech took photos. Stanton glanced at her back; it was filled with the circular burn patterns.

"ME will be able to tell us more," Stanton said. "I'd like his preliminary autopsy report as soon as it's done, as well as any forensics reports."

"You got it," Erin said. "Anything else?"

"Yeah," Gunn interjected. "Keep your gun next to you at night."

CHAPTER 30

Emma Lyon stood at the head of the classroom and watched the clock. The exam was the second of the year and the most difficult one she gave. On a first exam, the students would be frightened enough. By the third and final exam, apathy and a full semester of work would wear them down. But the second exam was the great test. They would be overconfident from the first exam, assume they knew what was coming next, and then be thrown off by the difficult and esoteric questions. They would be unsure what was coming, and any apathy would be shaken away.

The exam was focused on entropy and Gibbs free energy. The topic made her uncomfortable; she was never one to see science as a closed system, and applying entropic principles to daily life was a frightening prospect. According to thermodynamics, thermal energy always flowed from regions of higher temperature to regions of lower temperature. The process reduced the state of order in the initial system, so, in a manner of speaking, entropy was the measure of chaos in a system. As the second law of thermodynamics showed, entropy only increased or stayed the same. It was never reduced.

When she'd first learned that principle, images of empires laid to waste, of entire species gone extinct, of space stations destroyed, of planets made uninhabitable filled her mind. She saw humanity as a species that was born, reached its apex, and began its slow decline into chaos and then extinction. It was a thought that stuck with her and made the actual subject much more difficult than it needed to be.

"Time. Please put your pencils down."

Groans of frustration and relief from the class of twenty. A few mumbles came up about the pure difficulty of the exam, and more than one person predicted failure.

"You can turn in your sheets on my desk. I'll see you guys next week. We'll begin modules fourteen and fifteen, so make sure to have those read."

The class filed out, and she sat down at the desk, gathered the sheets together, and put them in a folder. For just a moment, she considered throwing them away and assigning grades randomly to stress entropy's point. It would be poignant and humorous at the same time, but she felt few of her students would find it amusing. Instead, she just slid the folder into her bag and left the classroom. She decided she wasn't going to pick anything up from her office and would instead just head home.

It was a long drive on a freeway that was congested to the point of immobility. The radio reported four separate accidents, and officers were trying to clear them up as quickly as possible. She rolled down her window and leaned back in the seat, trying to calm herself as wafts of exhaust came into her car. Eventually she had to roll the window back up.

Her phone rang. It was Steve Cutler, the dean of the college of science.

"This is Emma."

"Didn't catch you at a bad time, did I?"

"No."

"I need you to cover that symposium next Thursday and Friday up there in San Francisco."

"Steve, I told you I can't do that. I have labs and a research thesis that's due for publication in just—"

"No excuses. Just do it."

"This is the third time you've sprung something like this on me. I don't see too many other tenured professors getting that."

"No one else can do it. Suck it up and go. You might like San Francisco."

"What is all this about? Is it because I told you to go home to your wife?"

"I was drunk when I did that. Women like you are a dime a dozen out here. Don't flatter yourself. Now go to that symposium and quit being such a pain in the ass."

He hung up before Emma could say anything else. She felt like throwing her cell phone out the window or punching her steering wheel. Instead, she decided she would have to go to the symposium and suck up the humiliation. She had played with the idea of a lawsuit, and now it seemed inevitable: Steve Cutler should not be supervising anyone, much less young women looking to rise up the career ladder.

By the time she got home, it was already dark, and the streetlamps were on. She parked in her garage and went inside. The salty tinge of the air so close to the beach had bothered her at first, but she had grown accustomed to it.

She opened a couple of windows to cool the house before kicking off her shoes and getting a bottle of wine out of the cupboard. She poured herself a full glass and sat down on the couch. She received a text from a friend of hers, Marcy, who worked with her occasionally as a volunteer with the fire department's investigation unit. The text told her to watch Channel 4 right now.

She turned on the television, and went to Channel 4. It was the news. They were running a story on a pile-up accident on the freeway involving six cars. She was about to change the station when the next story came up—it was about the arson investigation of two homes.

She saw the reporter standing in front of a burned-out ruin that used to be a home. Police were combing the area behind her. The reporter was speaking about the family: the Humbolts and their six children. Jon Stanton came on and spoke of the helplessness of the police. There was a photo on the screen now: a mother, father, and six children. The youngest was one and a half, and she was smiling and holding a stuffed animal. Then an elderly woman came on; she was weeping uncontrollably, holding a family photo, and trying to describe the last time she had seen her grandchildren. She kept repeating a phrase: "my babies, my babies."

Emma noticed a sensation on her cheek. She thought perhaps she had an itch but felt the sensation go further down. She put her hand to her cheek and realized she was crying.

CHAPTER 31

Dr. Jennifer Palmer sat across from her patient and wished she were anywhere but where she was right now. Most patients were manageable, and even the ones with acute neurosis were able to control themselves in her presence, but this woman was something else entirely.

She was young, twenty-five, and had deep lacerations running up her forearms. She was in the middle of describing a sexual encounter she'd had last night with an unknown male she had picked up at a club. She had begged him to defecate on her chest, and the man had complied.

Jennifer kept her eyes fixed on the patient, but her mind was a million miles away. She was thinking of another patient she'd had a few years ago; a jolly, overweight male in his fifties. He had begun to have chronic and unrelenting bouts of depression. He seemed jovial enough, and Jennifer thought the depression was a symptom of rage he was feeling at his current work and family life. Before she could get him on the appropriate medications of Xanax and Elavil, he had shot himself at four in the morning in his basement, in a corner where he kept an old rocker that he couldn't bring himself to throw out. Of all the things she could have wondered, only one thing kept coming back to her, and she didn't know why: did he set his alarm clock for four in the morning?

The girl was bragging about her proficiency at oral sex when the timer on Jennifer's phone vibrated in her pocket.

"That's our time for today, Brandy. I would like to talk more about this next time, but I did have a request for you: in the six days before you see me again, do you think you can try to stay out of clubs and bars? Do you think you could do that for me?"

"Why?"

"Call it instinct, but I think we may have treated your drinking and partying as a symptom when in fact they may have been the cause."

"What?"

She gave her a warm smile. "No bars, no clubs for six days. Can you do it?"

"Sure, I guess."

"Thank you. Okay, next week then."

Jennifer walked her to the doors leading to the reception area, and as she said goodbye she noticed Jonathan Stanton sitting on the couch. He was more casually dressed than normal: just a T-shirt and jeans with a black jacket. His head was bowed low, and he was gazing at the floor, unaware that she had just stepped out of her office.

"Jonathan, are you ready?"

"Oh, yeah. Sorry."

"No problem. Please, come in."

She shut the door as he sat down, and she slowly walked around the office, in the opposite direction of what would have been most efficient, and poured herself a glass of water from a jug into a paper cup. She sipped a few moments and then threw the cup away. She wished she'd had enough time between patients to take a rest, maybe go for a walk or watch some television or read. Anything to empty her mind of the thoughts imposed by the previous patient.

"How have you been, Jon?"

"Fine."

She sat down. "Tell me what's going on in your life."

"Nothing, really. It's getting more difficult to see my kids, but I guess that's expected when they're becoming teenagers, right?"

"Why would you think that?"

"They're more involved with friends than with their families."

"That's true for some teenagers, but from what you were telling me about your relationship with your sons, that doesn't sound like it's a normal occurrence for them."

"I think maybe my ex-wife has been lying to them about me. They don't look at me the way they used to. They're not excited to spend time with me."

"When one parent can only spend a fifth of the time they used to with their children, the children sometimes rebel. They protect themselves by trying to cut off their emotional attachment to that parent."

Stanton took a deep breath. "I think I may want to fight for custody. The divorce decree didn't give her full custody; it gave us joint legal and physical. We just agreed that, because of stability issues with school and friends, they would live at her house. I'm starting to regret that decision. I haven't seen them in five weeks. They've been at camp for two of those weeks, but still. I can't help but feel they're avoiding me. I want to fight for them."

"How do you think that will make your sons feel?"

"I don't know. Hurt, I guess. I've spoken to an attorney, and he says a good way to win is to paint the other spouse as unfit. We'll have to parade her string of boyfriends and frequent drinking in court. The kids will be there, they'll have to hear that."

"Have you tried just talking to her?"

"We can't talk anymore. And unless it involves child support payments, she won't return my calls."

Jennifer nodded. "How's your work?"

"I saw something the other day that disturbed me."

"Disturbed you how?"

"Well, it wasn't the thing itself, but the fact that I wasn't disturbed by it that bothered me, if that makes sense."

"Can you give me specifics?"

"A girl was cut up in her bedroom in a particularly horrific way. The other detectives, even the forensics guys, could barely look at her. I heard the responding officer had to go see the precinct counselor afterward."

"How bad was it?" She held up her hand. "Wait, I shouldn't have asked that, I'm sorry."

"It's fine. It was bad. You'll probably see something about it on

TV. It involved cannibalism, and that always makes the news."

"That sounds awful. Is there a reason you think you weren't bothered by it?"

"No. I mean, when I first walked into the bedroom and saw her remains, I was a little taken aback, just by the sheer gore of it, but then I was fine. Why do you think that is? That I'd be okay looking at something like that?"

"I would figure in your line of work you may grow desensitized to scenes of violence. What do you think the reason is?"

"I wish it was that."

"Sounds like you have a pretty good grasp of what it is."

"I think... when I see something like that, I can put myself in the victim's place, but that's not where my thoughts first take me."

"Where do they take you?"

"I see how she was picked, what made her special. I see... lust for her. I felt what he probably felt when he first saw her."

Jennifer crossed her legs but didn't say anything. After a long while, the silence became somewhat unbearable. This was normally one of her favorite periods in a session; patients needed to fill that silence, and without any forethought, they would babble. The babbling was the purest picture into their subconscious mind that Jennifer had. But Stanton didn't respond that way. He just sat quietly and waited, to the point that it made *her* uncomfortable.

Suddenly, he stood up. "I think I don't want any more counseling today."

"Jon, wait a minute. Please, sit back down. I'd like to explore this."

"Not today." He turned and left.

Jennifer took a deep breath and then stood up. She went and sat at her desk and scribbled down a few notes about the session. There was something underneath Jon Stanton's exterior that was captivating. Her gut told her it might even be dangerous.

CHAPTER 32

Stephen Gunn pulled up to the apartment complex and jumped out with such glee he nearly hit his heels together like some leprechaun. He sprinted up the stairs to Jaime Spencer's door. It was locked, and he used his key rather than knocking and waiting for her.

"Hello?" he said, going in.

The apartment was actually clean for once, with vacuum impressions on the carpets. He went to the fridge and took out a beer, drinking half of it down before noticing the note on the counter. He walked over and picked it up:

Stevie, make yerself at home I'll be back later Jamie

He crumpled it up and threw it in the garbage. She had probably gone out to score and would stumble back at one in the morning, used up from what she'd have to do to score enough H or OxyContin to keep her high for the next few weeks. Gunn wondered what the hell he was doing with someone like her.

He went into the bedroom and lay down on the bed. He closed his eyes and listened to the traffic outside. Kids played, chasing each other with water balloons and squirt guns.

Gunn had never been able to play games like that when he was a kid. His father, when he was actually home, was so drunk that Gunn had to intentionally piss him off in order to get a beating. His father was fat and a pothead; he didn't have the energy for two beatings in a night. If Gunn could take it, he'd spare his mother and younger sister. But Gunn had been sickly as a child, and many of the beatings broke bones and tore ligaments. He would have to live with the injuries until morning, when his mom could take him to the emergency room and spend the co-pay without his father blowing up.

The last time Gunn had seen his father, one moment had almost made those years of pain worth it. In that moment, he let his father know who he was. He beat him for over an hour, so badly that his father had passed out several times. Gunn sat down on their cigarette-stained sofa and patiently waited for him to wake before continuing. Gunn had been sixteen years old.

A sound came from the living room as Gunn dozed off to sleep. It was soft, almost a scratch, and if the kids had been yelling or a car had been driving by at that moment he wouldn't have heard it. He thought perhaps a dog or cat was clawing at the door, and he thought about getting some food out for the animal; he could use some company right now.

Then, he heard a click. The doorknob began to twist. The door opened quietly, only a minor creak as it closed again.

Instinctively, he jumped to the floor and crawled under the bed, pulling out his Glock and aiming out the bedroom door. Jaime wouldn't have been so quiet, couldn't have been so quiet.

The footsteps in the hall were light, light enough that he couldn't hear them until they were close. Then he saw a pair of Converse shoes stop in front of the bedroom and then keep going farther down the hall. They came back a minute later and walked to the bedroom closet, opened it, and then closed it again. The bed above him dipped down as the person sat. Gunn heard the beep of a phone, and then a male voice said, "Yeah, he ain't here. Nah, I'm tellin' you, the motherfucker ain't here."

Gunn, as quietly as he could, moved his head enough to peek out from under the bed. The man was still talking on his phone, turned away from Gunn. Across his lap rested a 12-gauge shotgun.

Gunn slowly pulled his Glock up across his chest and out from under the bed. He was just slowly going past the metal railing when the barrel tapped the bed from an inadvertent muscle twitch. The man immediately looked down, saw Gunn, and went for the shotgun on his lap.

Gunn fired two rounds. One hit the man in the side as Gunn slid back under the bed, and a shotgun blast went off into the floor. Gunn rolled out on the other side of the bed and fired three rounds to keep the man on the other side of the room. He got to his knees and fell back down as another blast echoed off the walls.

On the floor, Gunn aimed for the man's ankles on the other side of the room. He steadied his hand and fired. A scream as the man nearly toppled over. He stumbled out of the room, blood trailing on the carpet.

Gunn jumped to his feet and went after him. He glanced out the bedroom door and saw that the man hadn't waited for him. He was already out the front door. Gunn ran after him, but by the time he was at the front door, the man was hobbling to a waiting car. Gunn lifted his weapon but didn't fire at him. Instead, he shot one round into the front tire, and then another round into the rear tire, which seemed to explode from the sudden release of pressure. The driver got out and ran, and the man who had been in the apartment turned with his shotgun aimed at Gunn's chest.

Gunn dove behind the railing as it shattered, the plastic in between the metal bars spraying over him in sharp fragments. He fired two rounds, missing both times as shards of the plastic had cut up his face and gotten in his eyes. He rolled backward as far as he could go until he hit a storage closet used by the unit across from Jaime's. When he tried to stand, his knees buckled, and he fell to the floor with a thud. Finally, he noticed the small holes dotting his chest.

His breath was short, and he felt as though he were about to pass out. He got out his cell phone and dialed 911. By the time dispatch answered, he had blacked out.

CHAPTER 33

Stanton raced down the freeway. He weaved in between cars, and when he couldn't weave, he honked and rode their butts and blared his sirens—two small red and blues attached to his windshield and rear window—until they moved. It took him ten minutes to make the drive down to Scripps Mercy Hospital that should've taken him twenty. He parked in emergency patient parking and ran inside, flashing his badge quickly to the nurse and demanding the room for Stephen Gunn.

"He just barely left the ICU. Visiting hours aren't until—"

"I want to see him now."

"Sir, I can't let you—"

"Who're you going to call if I force my way in and look into every room? The cops? I am the cops. So just give me his room, and you'll save both of us hours of wasted time."

The nurse didn't budge at first and then picked up a chart on a clipboard. "He's in room 162."

Stanton walked quickly down the hall. He passed several rooms with patients lying quietly and watching television. He got down to 162 and peered in at Gunn staring blankly out the only window in the room.

"What the heck happened?" Stanton said.

"I'm not tellin' you," Gunn said, his voice hardly a whisper, "until you actually swear."

Stanton sat down on a stool next to the bed. "What's going on, Stephen? Why were you at the complex?"

"Just getting some pussy, you know me."

"Who?"

"Just a girl. It don't matter, you don't know her."

"Who did this to you?"

"I don't know. Some black dude."

"'Some black dude'? Did you actually go through police training?"

Gunn attempted a laugh and then grimaced in pain. "Don't make me laugh. It fuckin' hurts."

"Who was it? This wasn't random. They found a slip of paper in the car you shot up, with your name and that address on it."

"No shit? Coulda fooled me. This city nowadays, you can't control the violence. I blame video games."

"I'm serious, Stephen. Who did this to you?"

"It's none of your business. I can deal with it."

"I can help if you let me. You're going to be in here another week, at least. You got buckshot in your shoulders and upper chest. It barely missed your heart. Someone needs to be out there following up on the car. Let me help you."

"You fuckin' Mormons. I swear you'll never learn that some people don't want your help. We just want to be left the hell alone."

"To get shot up again? What if I'm there next time, and they hit me too? What about if it's in a crowded place and there're kids? No, nuh uh, you tell me right now what you know."

"It's nothin' I can't handle, Jon. You got enough shit to worry about. Focus on them cases we still got open."

Stanton stood up. "Fine, you won't help me, I'll follow up on my own."

As Stanton was walking out Gunn yelled, "You got one week, Brother Jon. After that, I'm outta here, and I'm on the hunt. If you want 'em, you better find 'em before I do."

In the afternoon Stanton went back to his office. He collapsed onto his chair, put his feet up on the desk, and flipped on some calming music. He closed his eyes for a long time and just listened before getting the distinct impression that someone was in the room with him.

He opened his eyes and saw Childs watching him.

"Thought you was asleep."

"Just resting my eyes. What's up?"

"Sorry 'bout Steve, man."

"It happens. We're not milkmen."

"Does he have any idea who did this?"

"I don't know. You'll have to ask him."

"Oh, I see, 'protect the partner' and all that shit. Well, your partner's got some fucking serious enemies, Jon. You better recognize what that could mean for your health, too. Don't take no chances. Find out what's going on. He respects you. He'll open up."

"I'm not sure that's true, but thanks."

As Childs left, Stanton turned to the folders that were neatly arranged on the credenza behind him. Now that he was officially off the arson cases, he had been assigned several new ones, run-of-the-mill homicide: drug deals gone bad, a botched robbery, and a drive-by shooting that had struck a seventy-one-year-old man in a wheelchair and missed the target completely. He reached for one of the files and then stopped. He reached under his desk to a drawer and pulled out the copy of the arson files he had made before handing them off to the lead detectives.

He stared at the photos of the two families. The children in both families were young, and they had met a type of madness that few even knew existed. He wondered what they would have become if they'd been given the chance. Some of them would have been successful. Some of them, mediocre. Some strung out on drugs and living on the street. Perhaps one of them would have even become the type of monster that snuffed out their lives, or the cop chasing men like him.

"Jon?"

He looked up. A receptionist stood there with some papers. "Yeah?"

"Fax just came in for you. It's from Erin, Stephen's ex."

"Oh, right. Thanks."

Stanton took the forensics reports and laid them on the desk, reading the note that the autopsy had just been finished and the preliminary report for that would be coming. On the last page was a police sketch.

Several neighbors had seen the man coming and going from the Gaspirini home, so Erin felt the sketch was relatively accurate. The man on the paper was bald with a chiseled jawline and a slim nose. He would probably be handsome, in life. Stanton looked at the eyes a long while. They were set just a bit too close, and the sketch artist had drawn them with the lids partially down. They were the eyes of a corpse, empty.

The truth was he had completely forgotten about Monique Gaspirini and that he had promised to help Erin with this case. She was new to Homicide and still trying to prove herself. He knew she had called Gunn just to get Stanton there. He had a reputation for cases like these. Once, there had even been a newspaper article with an anonymous source in the San Diego PD calling him psychic. After that, the floodgates of grief opened up. Families would show up at the precinct unannounced with photos and personal items of loved ones who had gone missing with no leads as to their whereabouts.

Mothers would come in and weep, and Stanton would be too softhearted to turn them away. He would give them Kleenexes and sit across from them as they discussed what their son or their daughter liked to do, how kind they were, how many friends they had. They would describe birthdays and vacations and how full of life their children had been. They begged him to pick up their child's brush or their favorite pen or their shoes and find them. They asked him to speak to the dead, to call upon Christ, to perform séances.

Every time, he would have to give them the same speech: he wasn't psychic. He did the same things every other homicide detective in every other county in the country did. He had just gotten lucky a few times, that was all. And every time, he would have to watch as the parents' hearts broke in his office as they quietly gathered their children's items and left.

Stanton closed his eyes and took a deep breath, pushing the thoughts and memories out of his mind. When he opened them again, he put away the arson files and began reading about the death of Monique Gaspirini.

CHAPTER 34

Amber Rose Hill lay under the covers, waiting for direction. The three men in the room stood by the video and audio equipment, and there was another woman adjusting the lights. This was amateur stuff, and she regretted having to do it. The co-star, Bobby Stud, was nude and being fluffed in a corner by a girl who was new to the business.

"Are we gonna finish this or what?" Amber said.

"Doesn't look like it, hon," the director said. "Having some issues with the video. We'll have to reschedule."

She groaned. "I got shit to do all this week, Jimmy."

"I know, sweetie, but what do you want me to do? We need tech support to come in here and fix this shit. Unless you know how to fix a twenty-thousand-dollar camera, we're cancelling."

She got out of bed and found her pink robe on a chair. She put it on and headed back to the dressing rooms. The fluffer was still hard at work, and Amber said, "You can stop sucking his cock now, shoot's over," as she walked by.

She shared the small dressing room with all the other actresses. Bras and panties and costumes were thrown over the furniture and floor. She found her clothes and purse in the closet, dressed, fixed her hair, and left.

Her BMW came to life as she turned the key and she backed out of her stall and slipped on her Dolce & Gabbana sunglasses. This film had been a disaster from the beginning, and she was pissed. It'd been three weeks of shooting, and they weren't even halfway done yet. Jimmy, the director, was a film school dropout and wanted to get all creative. He was always over budget and short on time. If the money hadn't been so good, ten grand for what was looking like five weeks' work, she'd have bailed long ago.

Her cell phone rang; it was Jessica, her sister.

"Hey, Jess."

"Hey. What're you doin'?"

"Just leaving work. What're you doing?"

"Same. You wanna grab some coffee or something?"

"Yes, please. I'm in such a fucking bad mood right now."

"Where you wanna meet?"

"That bookstore by my house. What's it called?"

"Phil Weller's."

"Yeah, meet me there. I flirt with the coffee guy and he gives me the drinks for free."

"All right. Gimme ten minutes."

Fifteen minutes later, Amber was still stuck on the freeway. She blared some Pussycat Dolls on the stereo as some guys in the car next to her kept trying to get her attention. She made a note in the calendar on her phone that she would have to get her windows tinted.

By the time she got to Phil Weller's, her sister was already at a table, sipping a latte. She was flipping through a few books, and her legs were crossed, revealing perfectly tanned thighs. She would've made a hot adult film star, Amber knew, and several times she'd asked her sister if she wanted to try a scene or two. She always refused, and instead had enrolled in the University of San Diego to study computer science.

"Hey, sorry, traffic was a nightmare."

"That's okay. Is that boy here?"

Amber glanced around. "Yeah, hang on." She went and flirted for a few minutes and got coffee with two pastries and came back to the table. She took a few sips as her sister flipped through the pages of a book.

"I don't know if I like this anymore," Amber said.

"Like what?"

"You know, the business."

"I told you you wouldn't," Jessica said. "You're a whore with a camera in the room."

"Hey, don't be such a bitch."

"Sorry, I didn't mean it that way."

She sipped her coffee. "How're mom and dad?"

"Call them and ask."

"They don't want to talk to me."

"They would love to talk to you, Am. They just don't understand why you're doing what you do. Dad said he was at work, and in the break room was this calendar with you in it. You were August or something. He said you were totally naked and shaving yourself in a shower."

She blushed. "He saw that?"

"What did you think would happen? That no one you knew would see you naked? Everybody's seen it. All the young boys at church look you up online, and then their parents call mom and yell at her like it's her fault."

"I just kinda fell into it, ya know? Like, I started stripping, and I was making good money, and this guy offered to—"

"I know the details, and I don't believe you. It's *easy*. You just suck cock and then bend over and you're done. It's much easier than going to school and getting a real job."

"You don't think this is a real job? I work eighteen-hour days sometimes."

"It's not work, Am. It's just not, I'm sorry."

They were quiet a long time, glancing around and sipping their drinks. The silence was filled with the sound of turning pages in Jessica's books. Amber took one of them and opened it up. She read two entire pages before closing it and standing.

"I'm going to look around a minute."

Her sister nodded but didn't say anything.

The bookstore had three stories. The basement was for used books, the main level for new bestsellers, and the third floor for new obscure books, like philosophy and literary analysis. She went downstairs, and to her right was a display of books about modern art. A man was reading a book on Marcel Duchamp. He was dressed impeccably, dark-colored jeans with a blue button-up and a black silk scarf. But there was something off about him. The skin on his face looked red, and portions of it were peeling, as though he'd had a bad sunburn. His eyebrows and eyelashes were gone, and he was bald. He looked up at her and smiled. She smiled back to be polite; he was handsome, but probably too young for her and without much money. She turned her attention to the books, absently walking down an aisle and picking one off the shelf.

As a girl, she had loved books, and she remembered one summer in junior high at her parents' summer ranch when she had read fifty of them. Most were teen fiction, but she had thrown in some history and literature for good measure. Her plan had been to become a teacher, something her parents despised. Her father had been pushing her to go to business school, as he had. He had a legacy at Wharton, and two of her three brothers had gone there before starting work at her father's computer assembly plant. But things hadn't worked out that way.

Was what she did really so bad? People had sex every day, and most people who didn't were the ones who didn't have anyone else to have it with. Why was it so bad for her? Especially when she made a ton of money doing it?

"They're going to be remaking that."

She turned around. The man from the modern art display was standing a few feet from her.

"Excuse me?" she said.

"*Cosmos* by Carl Sagan. The book you're holding. They made an excellent documentary series based on that book, and the series is going to be remade. I suppose everything needs to be remade every so often. People change so quickly."

"I've never really been interested in cosmology."

"Are you religious?"

"How did you guess?"

"Religious people usually feel they have the answers to life's biggest questions, and they miss out on asking them."

"So you're not religious, then?"

"I read a story once, long ago, about a church that was set on fire with children inside. They were there to make packs of goods to send to troops overseas. None of the children could get out, and they burned to death. It seems the innocent suffer the most. I don't know if a god, at least no god I would want to worship, would allow that."

"Maybe it's part of his plan. Even evil has a purpose." She

replaced the book on the shelf. "It was nice talking to you," she said, emphasizing that the conversation had ended.

She glanced back, and the man smiled before turning around and heading up the stairs to the main floor.

It was two hours later when Amber got home to her upscale condo. Her sister had done little more than lecture her the whole time they were together, and she eventually made up an excuse and left. She hadn't felt like going home yet, so she went to the beach. Sometimes she would go there and watch the surfers for hours, the way they would glide on the water like birds. It looked so freeing. For some reason, she had never tried it and wondered why.

Unopened mail lay on the kitchen table, a nice marble she'd had imported from England, and she flipped through bills and opened the fan letters. Of course, she would never publicize her address, but the studio would occasionally forward fan mail that caught their attention and they thought demanded a response, such as if a business magnate in New York wanted to hire her for a night on the town, or a bachelor's party at Yale requested that she be their entertainment. This was the real way people in the adult business made their money—outside of the studio. But she could never bring herself to do most of what was requested of her. She would politely decline and let the studio know not to forward such mail to her again, but they always did.

Amber took a long shower, the hot water running over her body and relaxing her muscles. She used a loofa to cleanse herself and toweled off before putting on a silk robe as she stepped into the kitchen. She went to the sink and took a few vitamin pills out of containers. She glanced up through the window over the sink. The man from the bookstore stood there, a grin on his face as he bowed his head.

She screamed and dropped the glass. The phone was right behind her on the wall, and she grabbed it as she heard glass shatter behind her. She got the numbers in, but before the phone could dial out, she felt a hot impact against her head, and the next thing she saw was the floor as it rushed toward her.

CHAPTER 35

Jon Stanton sat in the pew at his local Mormon ward with his head bowed. It was a fast and testimony meeting. Once a month, the members were asked to fast during the day and pray and ask the Lord for something—for themselves or their families if they required it but mostly for others. The money they saved on meals would be given to the poor. Then, at Sacrament meeting, the Sacrament would be passed, and the time would be turned over to the members to come to the podium and bear their testimony. That meant anyone could get up and talk about whatever they thought was relevant.

Most of the members discussed small miracles they had seen in their lives and didn't feel there was any explanation for other than God's hand.

Stanton's eyes closed, and he felt himself slipping into sleep. He leaned back and stretched his neck. The past four days had been a blur. He had followed up on the car that was left behind at the scene of Gunn's attempted murder. It belonged to a woman in Watts who the

LAPD couldn't locate. The shells for the shotgun were bought from Wal-Mart. The gun itself probably was, as well. A young man had checked in to a hospital with two gunshot wounds that day, but it was in Los Angeles, and by the time word got down to SDPD, he was already gone.

Stanton had also followed up on Monique Gaspirini, interviewing neighbors and going over the crime scene video, painting a picture of the type of person who would do something like that. As far as he could tell, it was the worst type of offender: a sexual sadist. Most murders of this sort were either rage or sexually motivated, but a sexual sadist was both rage *and* sex. It was the most dangerous type of personality disorder that Stanton dealt with.

He remembered a case of a sexual sadist who had kidnapped a young college student and tied her to the ceiling of his basement for torture. She had died early from a heart attack, perhaps surviving no more than ten minutes. The sadist had been so enraged, he beat her corpse with his fists for over half an hour. Flustered, he'd dragged the body out in broad daylight, and a neighbor had called it in.

Stanton had been working eighteen-hour days without stop. Given that he spent at least an hour a day surfing, that left only five for showering, eating, dressing, spending time with his children, and sleeping.

Sacrament was over, closed with a hymn, but he hadn't noticed. He sat in the pew and waited until the rest of the congregation filed out before standing and following them. There were two more sessions, but he simply didn't have it in him to go. He decided he needed to get home and sleep before he passed out behind the wheel of his car.

As he walked out of the front doors of the building, a woman brushed past him. She stopped and turned and said, "Detective Stanton?"

He turned to her. She was middle-aged with a creased face and no makeup. A large purse was slung over her shoulder. "Yes?"

"I'm Jenna Pywe. You don't know me, but I've emailed you before. I got a response, but I just wanted to meet you in person. I hope you don't mind me coming here. I know you're Mormon and this was the closest Mormon ward to your house."

Stanton ignored the fact that she had just revealed she knew where he lived. He was too tired to question her. Besides, with the internet, anyone could find out anything about whoever they wanted.

"I'm on my way home. What do you need?"

She reached into her purse and came out with a photo. It was of a young girl, perhaps eleven or twelve.

"This is my Claudia. She's been missing for two years now. I called the detective from Missing Persons every Friday to check on her case, but eventually he stopped returning my calls. He sent me an email saying that the case was cold and there was nothing he could do until more evidence turned up." She thrust the photo toward him. "Please, I've heard things about you. I know you have the highest rate of solved crimes in all of San Diego. I read the interview in the *Tribune* that said some people in the police think you're psychic. Will you please help me?"

There was such deep sadness in her eyes that Stanton could tell the pain was as fresh as the day she realized her child was missing. It was the type of pain that consumed everything in its path and left nothing behind. In the creases of her face, Stanton could see all the nights without sleep, the job she had been regretfully let go from, the isolation from family and friends. He saw all of this in just a few seconds, and there was nothing he could do about it. Right now, there was nothing left in him. His mental energy was completely spent, and all he could do was get home.

"I'm sorry," he said, without taking the photo. He turned and walked to his car, not looking back.

CHAPTER 36

Knocking at the door woke him again. It seemed distant, as if it were in his dreams. Stanton roused himself and listened. He heard it again. He rolled over and put the pillow over his head.

The knocking turned to doorbell-ringing. Reluctantly and with a loud sigh, he stood up, nearly stumbling over his nightstand, and walked out to the living room. He glanced at the clock on the oven as he went past the kitchen: 11:17 p.m. Stanton opened the door and saw Emma Lyon standing there in UCLA sweatpants and a sweatshirt.

"Can I come in?"

"Sure. How'd you get in, by the way?"

"I just waited until someone walked out of the front doors. Your building isn't very secure."

Stanton sat on the leather chair as Emma took a spot on the couch. She looked out the balcony's bay doors to the moon hanging in the sky.

"I love the view."

"Thanks."

"Would it be rude to ask how a cop affords a place like this?"

"Yes."

She smiled and he smiled back.

"I saw the news, Jon. I saw the family. The faces of the young girls who died in that fire."

"I'm sorry. I know it's not easy to see."

"I want you to know why I don't help the police. I'm not some anti-government nut. I have reasons."

"I'm sure you do. I'm not judging you, Emma. You have to do what you think is right."

"My father was wrongly executed. I have a hunch you already looked that up."

"Not me, but someone I know, yeah."

"It's something that doesn't leave me. I can completely understand how murder victims feel, but it's even worse than that. I wish he had been murdered because then I could just blame one person. But how do you blame bureaucracy? Do I blame the prosecutor who convicted him or the public defender who didn't lift a finger to help him? What about the judge who kept out good evidence or the morons in the jury?"

"I don't know who you blame, Emma. I don't have the answers." He leaned forward on his elbows. "But I know you can help keep that from happening to other people. Benny doesn't know what he's doing. Lord knows how many innocent people are sitting behind bars right now because of him. If I can close these cases and prove what an incompetent he is, those cases can be reopened and checked for errors. You could help with that. You could save people's lives."

She nodded and tucked her hair behind her ear. "I'm going to help you with these cases, and then I'm leaving San Diego. For good."

"Why?"

"Because you and others like you will keep coming to me with cases like this afterward. I'll never be left alone, and I won't have the heart or the excuse to say no. I'm going to accept a position at the University of Montana. No one will know my specialty or background. I'll just be another professor in a small town."

"Do you think you'll be happy doing that?"

"I don't know. But I know I can't do this anymore." She stood up and went over to him. She gave him a brief kiss on the lips and said, "Send me everything tomorrow." She walked out the door and was gone.

Stanton sat quietly. He went to the balcony and opened the doors and stepped outside. The air was warm and tasted salty. He sat down in a patio chair and watched the moon reflect off the waves.

Marine animals out there right now struggled desperately for life, the stronger ones eating the weaker ones. People assumed animals had no stress, but Stanton knew that wasn't true. On top of finding food and procreating, they also had to constantly look over their shoulders for the larger predator that was going to take them out. Few animals lived as long as humans for that reason; they simply had constant stress every moment of their lives. Stress, Stanton knew, was the great killer. He had no doubt that that was what would end his life and probably the lives of every cop in Robbery-Homicide.

He put his feet up on the balcony railing and relaxed on the chair. He was asleep again before he could think to get a pillow.

CHAPTER 37

At six in the morning, Stanton woke on his balcony. He got up and went back to bed and didn't wake again until nearly noon. Then he dressed in a wetsuit with shorts and had a light breakfast of cereal and a grapefruit before heading to the storage room that held his board.

The beach was packed with teenagers cutting school, mothers with their kids, tourists, and the self-employed who didn't feel like working today. He held his board vertically to minimize the space it took up and avoid hitting anyone with it. The sand was hot under his feet, and he realized he'd forgotten to wear his sandals.

The water was cold, much colder than the heat of the day let on. He paddled out as far as he could before running into the other surfers out on the water.

"Too cold, bro," one of the surfers said.

They paddled back to shore together, but Stanton lay on his board, letting the waves lift and drop him. He felt the rhythm of the ocean, its heartbeat, and he could've sworn that it matched his own. He felt as though he could get lost here, and no one would find him. For a brief moment, he envied those who were lost at sea for days or weeks. It was ridiculous, he knew, but for that moment he would've given anything to feel that silence and isolation.

He didn't notice he was shivering until his teeth began to chatter and he headed back.

Stanton arrived at the precinct around two in the afternoon and headed to his office. There were dozens of messages, and he went through them and returned some calls before having the receptionist make copies of the arson copies he had made and email them to Emma. The first home, the Brichards, had been cleared and declared an accident. It was no longer a crime scene, and Emma could visit it as much as she needed to. The second scene was still under investigation, and Stanton would have to be there with her for that one.

When he had finished returning his calls, he went down to the scene of the second fire, parked two blocks away, and left his car on. He could see the burnt-out shell of the Humbolts' home, but he ignored it and turned on NPR. It was a segment about the meaning of having a cat, and he turned it off.

He eyed the driver and the passengers of every car that passed. He was looking for someone specific. The cars were mostly full of young teenagers returning home from school, and they were speeding through the stop sign at the intersection so Stanton had to keep his eyes on the road to catch a good glimpse of them.

A red Camaro pulled to a rolling stop and turned the corner toward the house. In the driver's seat was a young man with red hair and a tight gray T-shirt. The passenger was Tabitha Richardson. Stanton pulled away and followed the car until it stopped in front of the Richardson's home. He got out and went to the passenger side window.

The window was rolled up, and Tabitha was making out with the boy. Stanton knocked on the glass, and she jumped. He suppressed a smile; she probably thought it was her mother.

"What do you want?" she said.

"I take it you remember me?"

"Yeah, so?"

"I'd like to speak to you for a minute."

"I'm busy."

"It won't take more than a minute. Please, step out."

"And what if I don't want to?"

"Then I may have to investigate why a boy who is clearly over eighteen is dating a fifteen- or sixteen-year-old girl."

"Who is this bitch?" the boy said.

"A cop," she said.

The boy's eyes went wide. "Um, maybe you better go with him."

She sighed and opened the door, shutting it behind her. "So, what do you want?"

"I'd like to know who you saw at the Humbolts' home the night of the fire."

"I told you, I didn't see anything."

"Tabitha, most of my job is trying to tell if someone is telling me the truth or lying, and you're lying to me. I don't want to ruin your life or get you in trouble or any of that. I just want the truth. Don't you care about the Humbolts? I hear they were very good to their neighbors."

She looked down at her shoes. "I used to babysit for them."

"I just want your help in finding who did this to them."

"My mom said that some of the cops were sayin' this was just an accident."

"It wasn't an accident. They were killed. And the person who did it is still out there, free to do it again. Tell me what you saw that night and help me catch him. Please."

She glanced back at the car to see what the boy was doing before folding her arms and leaning against the door.

"You can't tell my mom."

"You have my word."

"I was out with some friends. Some friends my mom don't want me to hang out with. I snuck out with them and we came back at, like, five in the morning. I went inside and then remembered I forgot my phone at a house we were at so I got back in the car with them and left."

"And what'd you see?"

"Some guy. He was standing in front of their house. He started walking away and I didn't think it was weird or anything. But then after…"

"Why didn't you tell me before?"

"I told you, I snuck out. My mom would kill me. I already failed math and was grounded forever. I didn't want to do that again."

"Do you remember what this man looked like?"

"Kind of."

"I need you to come down to the police station with me."

"Why?"

"I want you to spend some time with a sketch artist and give him a description of the man you saw. It usually takes just a little over an hour. You'll be back before dinner."

She rolled her eyes. "I wouldn't have said anything if I thought it was gonna be all this extra work."

"It won't take long, I promise. You can ride with your boyfriend and just follow behind me."

"Fine," she said, opening the door and climbing back inside.

Stanton leaned down and looked at the boy. "You're going to be following me to the police station. If you lose me, I'll assume Tabitha has decided not to help me, and I'll need to know how old you are, since you're dating a minor. Do you understand?"

The boy nodded.

On the way back to the station, Stanton considered turning the boy in for what was clearly a sexual relationship with an underage girl. But he seemed no older than eighteen or nineteen; the difference in their ages was minimal. He decided that if Tabitha gave him a working

sketch, he would let this slide.

CHAPTER 38

The Beaufort Street Army/Navy store was buzzing with activity as Jerry Stedwell clocked in and took off his jacket. He had been drinking that morning and knew he reeked of beer, but half the guys that worked there knocked back a few before coming to work. A lot of the guys worked part-time at both the store and the car wash next door. Jerry had gone there, and a few of them went out back and downed a twelve-pack before going back in.

"That was a long break," his manager and father, Dick Stedwell, said as he came into the break room.

"Just went and got somethin' to eat."

"Well, get your ass out there. Doug's the only one on the registers."

Jerry nodded and walked past him, holding his breath. He made it as far as the floor before his dad grabbed him and whispered in his ear, "And if I catch you drinkin' on the job again, you're out on your ass. Son or no son. Got me?"

"Yeah."

Jerry went out behind the counter near the firearms display and asked a few people if they needed help finding anything. He showed them some pieces—nothing fancy, as most people nowadays were on a budget—and then went and sat on a stool.

It was a mistake working there. He had realized that the day he started. But his dad paid him twenty bucks an hour, and he took all holidays off. There were no other jobs he could get as a high school dropout that would pay him that much without making him risk his life.

He burped, the stale taste of flat beer coming up, and saw a man walk into the store. He was slim but somewhat muscular and wore a silk scarf wrapped around his neck. His bald head looked as though someone had taken a blowtorch to it, and his face was bright red. The man walked over, a big smile on his face.

"Can I help you find somethin'?" Jerry asked.

"Yes. I'm looking for some equipment, and my research told me you may have what I'm looking for."

"What d'you need?"

"I work with flammable materials in high-temperature

environments."

"Yeah, I can see the burns, man. You gotta be more careful."

"That's why I'm here. I need flame-resistant clothing."

"What kinda temperatures we talkin' about?"

"Over a thousand degrees."

Jerry whistled. "Man, only people that come in here for that are military guys. You in the military?"

"Something like that."

"Oh, I get it. Can't talk about it. Yeah, a lotta Special Forces guys come in here and buy stuff and can't really say nothin'. It's cool. Well, lemme show you what we've got." Jerry led him away from the counter and nearly to the back of the store, the man following quietly behind him. They turned a corner and went past oxygen tanks and climbing gear before getting to the fire-resistant suits. "How long you looking to spend in the suit at a time?"

"No more than an hour, probably a lot less."

"Well then, what you need are flatlock drop shoulder seams. They'll stop your skin rubbing against the suit and you won't chafe as easy. And if you're gonna spend that long in it, you'll want something anti-microbial too. The inside of the suits can get nasty quick, and you can't wash 'em. Do you care about high visibility?"

"What do you mean?"

"A lotta workplaces require high-visibility suits, so companies make 'em silver or yellow. But the black is cheaper 'cause not too many people get 'em."

"Black, please."

"With temperatures that high, you'll definitely want somethin' arc-rated. I think I know what you need."

They walked a little farther down the aisle, and hanging up was a long black suit that covered the body from head to toe. It had extra padding over the palms and soles of the feet.

"This here," Jerry said, "this is top of the line stuff. Like I said before, military stuff. It's got this cool mesh layering so you got four layers, but it don't feel like you're wearing four layers. It's self-extinguishing so it'll never melt or burn. It's really good stuff, too, 'cause it's had three treatments before it even leaves the factory. This bad boy here, you could walk on the sun with it."

"I'll take that."

"It's two grand, though."

"That's fine."

"So what do you do for your oxygen?"

"I haven't thought about it."

"You can't go into high temps without oxygen, man. You're crazy. We got some good masks and tanks right over here. They'll protect your face up to the temps you're lookin' at."

"I'll take those, too."

"Cool. Anythin' else?"

"No, that'll be fine."

Jerry gathered all the equipment and headed up to the front. He rang everything up: $2,723.17. The man paid on a credit card, and when Jerry asked him for ID, he showed an out-of-state driver's license. Jerry packed everything and handed it to the man.

"Thank you, you've been very helpful."

"You're welcome. Hey, you got any problems, you can call here any time and talk to my dad. He was a fireman. That's why we got all this shit."

"Thank you, I probably will do that."

Jerry watched the man leave the store and turned to another customer. *What a nice guy.* He wished all his customers were like that.

CHAPTER 39

Stanton stood outside the two-way mirror and watched the sketch artist work with Tabitha Richardson. He particularly watched the way she interacted and answered questions—with an air as if she were doing him a favor just by being in his presence. She was beautiful by conventional standards, with bright green eyes and golden hair, and her beauty would get her far in life, or it would destroy her. Stanton had rarely seen beautiful women who were mediocre. They would enter modeling, acting, gymnastics or other sports, and then marry well; or if they happened to have intellectual power as well, they would enter business, law, medicine, or other professional fields, their looks bolstering their resumes.

That was one path.

The other was one of early molestation and later abusive relationships laden with heavy drug use. Many times the two would be intertwined, and high-profile models who seemed to have their lives and careers in order would buy cocaine cut with baby laxative on street corners or marry the most abusive husbands they could find. They would become porn stars and strippers and prostitutes. When their beauty faded away, they would be left with an empty shell of what had once been a life. Stanton saw many of them in their fifties and sixties and still on street corners trying to coax johns into letting them in their cars.

Stanton thought how interesting it would be to conduct research on the effects of beauty in life. If ever he were to return to academia, he would have to keep that subject in mind.

Detective "Slim Jim" MacAfee strolled up next to him, a microwaved burrito in his mouth. He stood there chewing, the sauce and cheese dripping down his chin onto the floor.

"Who's that?" he said.

"That's the sole witness on your arson case, the Humbolts."

"Benny said the evidence is inconclusive on that."

"You believe him?"

"No. The bastard's lazy. I didn't read about a witness in the reports."

"She wasn't in them."

"How'd you find her?"

"I don't know. I just thought she knew more than she was telling me."

If Slim Jim didn't believe that answer, he didn't show it. He continued eating his burrito and sucked down a Sprite. Before he was done, the sketch artist gave a thumbs-up, stepped out of the room, and joined them behind the glass

"Girl's got a good memory. Saw this guy for no more than ten seconds at night but could recall the shape of his lips."

"Did you get a good print?"

"See for yourself."

Stanton took the drawing. His heart raced, and his guts tightened up like a fist. "Slim Jim, this girl's life is in danger. We're getting her into protective custody right now. Send some uniforms to her house. Her family's in danger, too."

Nehor Stark bounded up the stairs to the second floor, his flame-resistant suit swooshing as he jumped up the top three steps. He kicked in the first door on his right. It was a bathroom. He tore down the shower curtain and looked in the tub. He pulled open the drawers underneath the sink so violently they broke. He bashed his fist into the mirror, and it broke in a spider web of cracks.

The next room was the master bedroom. He pulled the covers off the bed and kicked over the mattress. He heard a sound and thought a dog or other family pet was in there with him but then realized he was grunting like an animal. He kicked over the dresser and ripped the closet doors off before rummaging through the clothes inside.

"Where is she!" he screamed at the top of his lungs.

Nehor went through the next bedroom and tore it apart. He ripped the framed photos and drawings on the walls down hard enough to make the glass shatter into pieces on the soft white carpet. He ran down the hall to the next room, another bedroom. He tore curtains away and shattered the plasma TV against the wall, mumbling, "Where is she?" to himself.

He tore their clothes off the hangers and ripped them apart. The echoing screaming he recognized as his own.

Finding nothing in any of the rooms, he jumped down the stairs and ran into the kitchen. He opened drawers, dumping their contents on the floor to find the largest kitchen knife he could and then went to the living room.

Gagged and tied together with polyester rope, the Richardsons were crying and squirming. Hal Richardson, the father, had a large wound on his head that was pouring blood over him, soaking the rope around his chest a dark crimson. He seemed faint, like he could pass out at any moment. Nehor went instead to Katie, the mother, who he had left untouched.

"Where is she?" he said, placing the tip of the knife against her throat.

Katie shook her head.

"Your whole family is going to die, and I'm going to make you watch. If you tell me where she is maybe I'll decide to let all of you live and just take her. Is that a deal?"

Katie broke down, her head lowered, tears streaming down her face. She nodded.

"Good," Nehor said, reaching over and taking out the cloth he'd stuffed into her mouth. "Now, where is she?"

"She's down the street at a neighbor's house."

"Which neighbor?"

"Are you going to harm them?"

"No," he said, frustrated. "Now which fucking neighbor?"

"Six doors down. The Taylors."

He pulled the knife away. "Thanks."

Nehor jumped to his feet and went to the three red canisters that lined the wall on the south side. He began emptying the remnants over the floors and tracing a pattern into the hallway.

"Why are you doing that?" Katie cried. "You said you would let us go!"

"Did I? I don't remember."

She screamed as he finished the hallway and came inside, pouring the clear liquid over her two children and her husband. He went to retrieve another canister when he saw movement outside, in front of the house. It was a police cruiser.

He stood frozen, staring out the window as two officers got out of the car. They could be going anywhere, he thought. Then they walked up the yard and onto the front porch and rang the doorbell.

He didn't move. He didn't even breathe. He couldn't survive going back to living in a cage. He would die here, then, with this family and the two officers. He would set the fire so that it would cause an explosion as soon as the officers got through… no. No, why should he do that when there was a perfectly good back door?

Nehor glanced at the family as he ran past them. Briefly, he considered slitting their throats before leaving, and he took a step toward them. As he did so, one of the officers pounded on the door and said, "San Diego PD, please open the door."

Nehor's face twitched in anger. He threw the knife as hard as he could at Katie, the handle hitting her in the head and causing her to scream. He laughed so hard he nearly fell over.

He ran out the back door into the dwindling evening light. He jumped into a neighbor's yard over their fence and then ran to the street where Amber's car waited for him.

CHAPTER 40

"This is fucking bullshit!"

Stanton ducked a can of cola as Tabitha threw it at him. He approached her and grabbed her arms, sitting her down on the couch in the lounge. He stood over her as she folded her arms and sat back, anger raging in her face.

"It's for your own safety. And if you throw anything at me again, you'll be sitting in a cell instead of in the lounge."

"Good. I don't give a shit. Put me wherever you want."

"It's almost six o'clock. Is your family all going to be home at this time?"

"Fuck you."

He bent down, looking her in the eyes. "Tabitha, I'm trying to save your life and the lives of your family. Now please, it's very important. Is your family going to be home?"

She snorted. "Yes."

There was a knock at the door. Childs opened it and stepped

inside. He shut the door behind him so no one could hear and walked over, glancing down at Tabitha before turning to Stanton.

"The family's at Scripps Hospital right now. They're safe, but they were found tied up in the living room."

Stanton looked at Tabitha, and her eyes went wide as she realized which family they were talking about.

"He came to my house?" she said quietly. "That guy came to my house?"

Childs said, "He almost killed your family. Jon Stanton just saved your life. Maybe a thank-you is in order instead of throwing shit at him."

Childs turned and left as Tabitha stared blankly at the walls before tears ran down her cheeks. She put her hands to her face and began to cry. Stanton sat down next to her and calmly waited until she was ready. A moment passed before she leaned over on his shoulder. He let her cry it out, and when she had regained control of herself, he stood up.

"I'll take you to your family."

They drove in silence all the way to the hospital, and Stanton parked in handicapped parking before walking her to the ER. Her family was gathered in the same room, the father in a bed with a bandage around his upper skull. The rest of the family sat quietly until they saw Tabitha. She ran to her mother, and they hugged and cried. Stanton stepped out of the room.

A uniform sat in a chair outside, reading a *Rolling Stone* and not paying attention to what was going on. Stanton leaned down in front of him so he could see his eyes.

"The man who's after this family, he won't care that there's a policeman outside the room. Do you understand?"

"Yeah."

"Don't let them out of your sight. If they want to go home, tell them they can't yet and that they'll have to sleep in a hotel. Don't even let them in to get clothes. He may have wired the house with explosives."

"I won't let anything happen to them, Detective."

"I know you won't. Thank you."

As he was already here, Stanton decided to visit Gunn. He went up to his floor and walked into the room without knocking. Gunn was lying in the bed, staring up at a television blaring a game show. Stanton pulled a chair next to the bed and sat down. Gunn didn't move or say anything.

After a long while, he finally said, "You bring me anything?"

"Like what?"

"Like some beer? I can't get any booze in here."

"You know I wouldn't buy that for you."

"I know. Just thought I'd ask." He exhaled. "You look like shit, Johnny. You gettin' enough sleep?"

"No."

"Me neither."

Stanton leaned back in the chair and put his feet up on the edge of the bed. He watched the television. A woman in a tight dress answered that the capital of New York was Manhattan and lost all the money she had made. A young boy to the right of her shook his head in amazement.

"Did you mean what you said, Stephen? That you're gonna go after the people who put you in here?"

"If I say no, will you stop askin'?"

"Probably not."

"Didn't think so."

"I'm chasing down the owner of the car. It belongs to a woman who by all accounts has disappeared. I think if I can find her, though, I can find the men who shot you."

Gunn shrugged. "I ain't too worried about it."

Stanton removed his feet from the bed and leaned forward. "There's lines that once we cross they disappear, Stephen. They won't be there anymore, and we just end up becoming exactly what we hate."

"Thanks for the advice, Ma."

Stanton rose, placing his hand on Gunn's forearm. "I'm your partner. I'm here. You don't have to do this alone."

"What the fuck? What, are we on a fuckin' date or somethin'? Get your hand off me, Jon. I ain't gonna do shit 'cause I don't know shit. I know about as much as you do about who shot me."

"You're lying. I can tell."

"The world ain't black and white, good and evil, all right? Get off your Jesus complex bullshit and come down to earth with the rest of us."

"Jesus saved my life, Stephen. Do you believe me when I tell you that?"

"Sure, why not? Weirder shit's happened." He coughed. "Ah, my fuckin' ribs. You're aggravatin' me, man. I think I should get some rest."

"If you need anything, you call me."

Gunn sighed. He held up his hand, knuckles out, and Stanton bumped it with his. "I'm sorry. I didn't mean to be an asshole."

"Can't change who you are," Stanton said.

Gunn shrugged. "Keep me up to date on that arson shit, will ya? It's been on the news."

"I will."

"And be careful. This guy sounds like one sick fuck."

CHAPTER 41

Emma Lyon waited at her office until darkness fell before she rose from her desk and headed out the door. She had a full day of lectures tomorrow, but she would regurgitate old lectures she had already prepared or just do it by heart. She had given every lecture so many times that she occasionally dreamed about it and ran through the entire semester before waking, tired and groggy, early in the morning.

She heard footsteps behind her as she walked down the corridor out to the parking lot and turned to see Philip Christensen come out of a lab and smile as he saw her. He caught up to her, sipping on a Mountain Dew Code Red and stopped a moment to tie his shoelace.

"You comin' to that symposium?" he said.

"No, I don't think so."

"Why not?"

"'Cause we work for an asshole."

"So? You're tenured. Just come and see what he does."

"What he'll do is give me all the 7:00 a.m. classes and channel the funding to other people. He can't fire me, but he *can* turn me into little more than a TA."

Philip took a long drink. "Fuck it. It's still better than a real job."

"That it is."

They got outside and said goodbye as Emma got into her car. She put a Mozart CD into the player and waited until the music came on before pulling out of the parking lot and onto Springhill Drive. She turned west and then onto the interstate heading southeast. It was jammed with cars, their taillights like glowing red orbs hanging in darkness. Construction had blocked one of the lanes, and it was stop-and-go traffic for almost half an hour before she got off the nearest exit and took side streets to Harvard Avenue. Down half a block were the burnt-out remains of the Brichards' home.

She parked across the street and finished listening to the piece that was playing. Then she checked her digital recorder before slipping it into her pocket and getting a flashlight out of her glove box. She looked at herself in the mirror and took a deep breath before stepping out of the car.

The air was warm, and she thought it odd that that was the first thing she noticed. She glanced up at the full moon. It appeared brighter than usual, and she thought it must've been the fact that there were so few streetlamps in this neighborhood to provide light pollution.

She glanced around the neighborhood to make sure no one was out watching her. Though it had been found to be an accident, many of the neighbors had probably heard Stanton on the news describing it as arson, and they would be jumpy. Many of them would be armed and inexperienced and might take a shot at her, thinking she was a prowler. She waited near a telephone pole until she made sure that no one in any of the surrounding homes was watching her through the windows.

She went up to the porch, one of the only parts of the house that was still standing. She noticed a melted barbeque right next to a pet bed where the blankets had been charred but not burned. Fire was odd that way. It seemingly chose its targets. Emma had seen video of fires that had been set by arson investigators across the country, and when run at a slower speed, she could watch the flames zip around the house, up the walls, over furniture. And then, for no apparent reason, it would skip something like a lamp or a table. It would shoot over or around it. Investigators didn't pay much attention to it and figured it simply had something to do with the flow of oxygen in the room and the flammability of the substances around the item, but it was unsettling to see on video. The fire seemed alive.

She took out her digital recorder and hit the record button.

"Brichards' home, July first, about 10:00 p.m. There's a little doggie bed on the porch. I didn't see any mention of a dog in the police reports. The medical examiner didn't make note of a dog with the remains of the bodies. What happened to the dog?"

She held the recorder low as she walked around the perimeter of the home. Normally, she would take photographs and measurements, but she skipped those. Benny, she assumed, at least had the competence to measure accurately.

Emma walked in through what had been the front door and slowly took in the home. She took out her flashlight and ran it slowly around the hallway and then the living room. She studied the baseboards and then squatted to see them more closely. She went back to the hallway and examined the baseboards that had been left and went over the bedroom, the kitchen, and the bathroom, as well. There were no puddle configurations indicating the use of an accelerant. She slipped out a small plastic container and a metal device that looked like a scalpel and took several pieces of the baseboards in the hallway, living room, and bedroom, put them in individual plastic bags, and placed them in the container. She examined pieces of broken glass in the bedroom and placed a few pieces of them in her container, as well.

There was little else she could do right now. Analyzing any secretions from the bodies and surveying body position and the types and locations of burns were much better indicators of arson than most inanimate material, but she didn't have those now, other than a few photographs in a file. She held the recorder up to her lips.

"Maybe I was wrong. There's nothing here now other than a few samples. I don't see any indications of purposely setting the conflagration, other than the position of the victims in the photographs. None of the victims were attempting to flee, which means they were probably tied up in some fashion. The bodies have already been buried, and I won't be able to get access to them to test for any rope or plastic restraints. Unless the labs come back with a miracle, I'll have to agree with the county's fire investigator that this is probably an accident."

Emma did one more walkthrough of what had been the Brichards' home and then returned to her car. There was a cat near the driver's side tire, and she knelt down and ran her hand along his back. He arched and began to purr.

She glanced back at the house. Her gut told her this was purposeful fire-setting, but the evidence didn't add up. It didn't help that most of the evidence she could have used was either buried in the ground or had been washed away with a direct spray of a hose. Inexperienced firemen rarely spotted the difference between arson and accident upon coming to a fire, and many times most or even all the evidence of arson was washed away before a fire investigator was notified of the scene.

Witnesses could tell her if there was an odor or if the fire took an unusual pattern—indications of the use of an accelerant, as was yellow fire with dark, black smoke. One of the easiest ways to recognize an accelerant was flames that burned directly from the floor, which most witnesses had no trouble identifying. She regretted that there were no witnesses here to give her a clear answer.

She rubbed the cat's head for a moment before getting into her car and starting the engine. She put the plastic container containing the samples on the seat next to her and stared at it. It was nearly eleven o'clock, and she had an eight o'clock class in the morning. But excitement tingled in her belly. It was so rare for a genuine puzzle to present itself in her world. She pulled away, careful to avoid the cat, and sped down to the freeway heading back to UCLA.

CHAPTER 42

Jon Stanton hung around the hospital lobby after he left Gunn's room. He didn't know what exactly he was expecting to happen, but it felt like the place he needed to be right now. He got a Diet Coke from the vending machines and sat at a table, slowly sipping out of the cold can and listening to the conversations around him.

One woman, older, was describing the stroke she had suffered. She sat in a wheel chair, her friend next to her, and they laughed about it over ice cream as if she had slipped on a banana peel and hurt her backside. Another table was filled with young girls in their late teens discussing the gunshot wound their friend was being treated for. Speaking in hushed tones, one of them mentioned that she knew where the girl lived who had shot at them.

Stanton ignored them and sipped his drink. He took a good half an hour to finish and then rose and walked back to the emergency room. The Richardsons were still there, but they were packing up to leave. He was going to stop in and ask about the man who had assaulted them, but the uniform came up before he had a chance.

"Detective, I'm takin' the mom and the kids to a hotel. Dad's not doin' so good. He's got brain damage. Doc said he might have permanent blindness in one eye."

Stanton glanced into the room. The young children sat with blank stares directed at the walls or floors. Only Tabitha had her eyes fixed on her father, who was lying back asleep on the hospital bed. Her eyes were rimmed red from crying, and he could see the spots on her skirt where the tears had fallen. She looked as though she still wanted to cry, but there was nothing left.

"I need to interview them," Stanton said. "I won't do it now, though. Tell them I'm coming by in the morning to speak with them. What hotel are you going to?"

"They ain't got much money with 'em. I was just thinking the Highway Lodge over there off Friar's Road."

"No," Stanton said. He pulled out his wallet and handed him a credit card. "Take them to the Marriott downtown. Stop at the grocery store first and make sure they have everything they need."

"You got it."

Stanton watched them leave without saying goodbye. He headed out to his car and got halfway down the corridor when his cell phone rang. He recognized the number as coming from the UCLA campus.

"Hello?"

"Jon, it's Emma."

"What're you doing up?"

"Nice to hear from you too."

"I didn't mean it that way. It's just late."

"I know you didn't mean it. I'm sorry. Look I'm calling about the Brichards' house. I went down and took some samples from the baseboards and the surface of the flooring. I tested it for accelerants."

"And?"

"Nothing. I was about to call it a night when I decided to run it through one more battery of tests in the spectrometer. Some compounds get burned off so efficiently that they're difficult to detect, so I had to analyze the wood itself rather than looking for accelerant on the surface. I found something."

"What?"

"It's not much, and I can only give you a range of probability as to the likelihood of its use, but I saw a trace amount of naphtha."

"What's that?"

"It's a somewhat broad term, and the exact composite varies with the manufacturer, but I think I saw a base of thinner. It would have to be nearly odorless and colorless. Something unique. Possibly something made to order."

"Who could make an accelerant like that for private use?"

"Well, if he's a chemist, he could make it at home. So we shouldn't rule that out. He could also just know somebody or have access to some laboratories that contain the compound. There is one other possibility: he could be with the fire department. They would have access to accelerants for training purposes."

"Let's hope that's not it." Stanton paused. "Is this something Benny should have picked up?"

"It was more difficult to find than other accelerants, but he didn't even test multiple samples. He took one and didn't find anything and declared it good enough. He needs to be fired, Jon."

Stanton walked outside to his car and leaned against it, watching the front entrance of the hospital as a man helped a woman in a wheelchair out. "Can you get me the lab results and a brief report?"

"Sure, I can email that to you right now."

"Thanks." He paused and then said, "I'm sorry about dinner."

"It's okay. It's… you didn't know."

"I'd like to make it up to you sometime."

"Sure, any time. You have my number."

"Thanks, Emma. I'll get back to you about this."

Stanton hung up and got into his car. He began to drive home and then made a quick stop at the beach to watch the moon reflect off the water. After a long while, he went back to his apartment and changed into shorts and a T-shirt and tried to sleep. As he drifted off, he pictured the final moments of the Brichards and Humbolts. He felt his throat tighten up, and he swallowed hard and rolled onto his side. He knew it would be another night without sleep.

CHAPTER 43

It was nine in the morning when Stanton came into the Northern Division, a manila folder under his arm, and walked by the front desk with a quick nod to the receptionist. He found Slim Jim with his feet up and earphones in, flipping through some reports in a brown file. Stanton lifted his earphones away from his ears.

"I'm meeting with Childs. I need you on this, too."

"What is it?"

"Arson cases."

Slim Jim rose and followed him to Daniel Childs's office. It was spacious but scarcely decorated. The only things up on the walls were a few medals and his Marine Corps drill sergeant hat, framed in a plastic case. Childs was reading over some documents on his computer and said, "Shut the door," without looking up.

Stanton shut the door as Slim Jim collapsed onto the old couch in the corner. He pulled a sucker out of his jacket pocket and unwrapped it, thrusting it into his mouth and folding his hands on his chest.

"So," Slim Jim said, "what's up?"

Stanton took out some papers from the file under his arm and put them on the desk. Childs's eyes went to them, and he began reading through him. Stanton didn't say anything until Childs pushed them away and looked up at him.

"I told you you were off these cases."

"I was right about them. I couldn't let it go."

"You were ordered to let it go."

"Fine, suspend me. But fire Benny and follow up on these." He took the two sketches out and placed them on the desk, Tabitha's sketch on top of the other. "This is him, Danny. He's targeting families and using an accelerant that most fire investigators can't detect."

Childs breathed heavily out his nose and lowered his eyes to the drawings. He glanced back up. "Slim Jim, you wanna keep these cases?"

"Hell no," Slim Jim said, picking a piece of lint off his tie.

"It's your case," Childs said to Stanton. "I'll find another body to partner up with you."

"Don't need it. I'll get Stephen when he gets out."

"You kiddin' me? He was shot, and you're gonna put him back to work?"

"I know him. He won't lay in bed long."

Childs leaned back in his chair. "All right, it's your show. You run it. But if you fuck it up and this is wrong, or if you're right and this… *thing* gets away, it's your ass."

"I know."

"So what's next?"

"I want to give these to the media and have them on the six and ten o'clock news and every website and blog we can."

"Tricky move," Slim Jim said, pulling the sucker out and looking at it as he twirled it in his fingers. "He could run."

"I know. I want a phone bank with as many people as we can spare. The calls'll come quick, and we need to nab him."

"What makes you say that?" Childs said.

"He's disorganized. He was so frantic to get work done at the Humbolts' that he let a sixteen-year-old girl ID him. He didn't care if the neighbors of the girl he cut up saw him. He didn't even bother to wear a wig or a baseball cap. The calls identifying him will come in quickly, and we need to have people on standby, ready to go as soon as we get the right call."

"I ain't got that many people, Jon. You can pull some interns and secretaries, but that's it."

"What about the trainees at the academy?" Slim Jim said.

Childs shrugged. "You call over and see if they can send them."

Slim Jim sighed as he stood up. "I wouldn't have mentioned it if I thought it was going to be more work for me."

Childs picked up the sketch. "Man, I hope you're wrong about this. I hope it was an accident. I don't wanna know that people like this exist in the same world as my daughter."

Within two hours, a room had been set up with twenty phones. Trainees had been pulled from their coursework at the academy on a volunteer basis, the volunteers having to make up the missed day on Saturday. Half a dozen interns from the local criminal justice programs at the city college joined them, as did two secretaries. Stanton had run to Kinko's and gotten the sketches blown up. He pinned them to the wall at the front of the room. Childs and Slim Jim came in and stood by as Stanton turned to the people sitting on the folding chairs at the long tables they'd taken from the cafeteria. Slim Jim nodded to him—

the sketches, as well as an official statement, had been sent to every media outlet in the county and even a few statewide.

"We're going to get a lot of people claiming to be him," Stanton said. "The accelerant he used was called naphtha. Ask them what type of accelerant they used in the fire, and if they say anything else, tell them the police are on their way to their location as we traced their number. They won't be, but we need to get them off the phones as quickly as possible and make sure they don't call back."

One of the trainees, a young man, raised his hand. "What if he answers right?"

"Let any of the detectives in the room know, and they'll run a trace on the call. He won't do that, though. He's too smart, and he hasn't shown any indication of wanting to make contact with us in the past." He glanced around. "Any other questions?"

"Yeah," one of the other trainees said. "Can I be the one to take the fucker for a ride when we catch him? I'd hate for him to get hurt by someone else's crazy driving."

There was a murmured, forced laugh from the crowd. Stanton smiled but didn't respond. He gathered a couple of pens and a legal pad, pulled out a folding chair, and sat at one of the tables, staring at the phone.

CHAPTER 44

Nehor Stark sat quietly in the recliner as the girl across from him woke up. He had cleaned and bandaged her head as well as he could with the supplies he'd found in the condominium. At present, the wound on the back of her skull had stopped bleeding, and he was confident she hadn't suffered any permanent injury. He didn't say anything as she came to and looked around the living room.

"Where am I?" she said, her voice thick with grogginess.

"You're home, dear."

"Who are you?"

"I'm your friend. Don't you remember?"

"No." She leaned her head back. "My head hurts."

"Would you like some medication? I found quite a stash of Percocet pills in your bathroom." He rose and took two pills out of an amber bottle on the coffee table. He held them up, and she opened her mouth without protest. He put them on her tongue and grabbed the plastic water bottle that was on a side table, putting it to her lips and allowing her to drink.

"What happened?" she said.

"Apparently you fell down and hit your head. Quite hard, I'm afraid."

"Shouldn't I go to the hospital?"

"Not yet, but you will."

"Who are you again?"

"Dear, I swear, you're going to start hurting my feelings."

"I'm sorry," she said, lifting her head only to have it collapse back down. "I don't feel good."

Nehor rose. "Get some sleep. I'll be back to check on you."

As he walked around the couch, he checked the cuffs on her ankles locking her to the chains that had been wrapped around the massive entertainment center. They gave her almost nine feet of slack, but it didn't matter. All the phones had been smashed, and the two entrances to the condo were at least twenty feet away.

Nehor stepped outside and got into Amber's BMW. It purred to life, and he pressed the accelerator a few times to hear the engine. He smiled to himself as he pulled out of the parking stall and onto Balboa Avenue. Pacific Beach wasn't far, and he briefly considered going there and putting his feet in the ocean. It'd been so long since he'd seen the ocean that he'd forgotten what it looked like. He had an image of it in his mind, but he knew it wasn't accurate any longer.

He drove for a long time and got on Interstate 15 for a while, putting the top down and enjoying the blasts of warm air over him. He pulled off when he spotted a police cruiser behind him and came to a quaint neighborhood he hadn't been to before. There was a yoga studio on one corner and a coffee shop next door with an alternative jewelry retailer across the street. He parked behind the yoga studio and went inside the coffee shop.

It never ceased to amaze him how much the styles of clothing had changed since he was young. Then again, his memories were little more than fragments, and even those had been altered in the time he'd spent in the little square room with no window. He didn't trust his memories to give him accurate information anymore, and he considered himself lucky. He was a man who wasn't bound to anything.

He ordered a coffee with milk and argued with the cashier who quoted him four dollars for it. He paid with a five and went to a condiment station, mixing in sugar with a thin straw before finding a seat by the window. He watched the passing traffic, the monstrous

SUVs and trucks that swallowed the road. Cars had gotten larger, more shiny, more a status symbol and less transportation. He remembered suddenly the smell of his mother's Buick as they drove from Nevada to California, stopping only once a day to eat at greasy fast food restaurants to save money.

A man sitting across from him at the next table was staring at him. Nehor caught his eye and smiled, and the man turned away. When he thought Nehor wasn't looking, he turned back, and then his eyes lifted to the television screen. Nehor glanced up to see a drawing of his face.

His heart began to beat in his ears, and the world seemed to slow. There was no sound, and the television had writing across it in white lettering, something he knew well but didn't know the name for. Many times, as punishment at the institution, they would turn off the sound to the television or leave the sound on and turn off the picture. They weren't allowed to starve or beat them, so it was the little things they used as punishment. He watched in amazement and phrases caught his attention.

...lead detective Jon Stanton... mass murder of... several fires in the La Jolla area... multi-jurisdiction manhunt... reward offered.

Jonathan Stanton. He spoke on the television, and Nehor watched him with wonder. He was lean and Caucasian with a light olive skin, as if part of his heritage was Mediterranean. He had soft eyes.

Nehor flipped over the table he was sitting at, to the shock of the patrons, before storming out of the coffee shop. One man tried to get in his way, saying something about the cost of the table before Nehor grabbed a glass bottle out of a girl's hand and smashed it into his head. The man instantly toppled over into a heap.

The sun was high and bright as Nehor hopped into his BMW and pulled away. Led Zeppelin, a band he was fond of, was playing, but the music was far away, and he didn't really notice it. There was only one thought on his mind now: *Jon Stanton.*

CHAPTER 45

Stanton checked the clock on the wall behind him rather than pulling out his cell phone. Six and a half hours had passed since he'd sat down and started taking calls. By his estimation, he'd handled over a hundred and fifty of them. Most were nutcases calling and pretending to be responsible for the fires or claiming they were married to the man in the sketch. A couple of callers asked if there were any female officers they could speak with, probably hoping to talk dirty.

But there was one call that stuck out: a fifty-one-year-old woman who believed that her son was the man in the sketch. Stanton pressed her, and she offered a few details. He was a loner at school and kept to himself at any social events. He seemed interested in girls, as the mother had caught him watching pornography several times, but he couldn't speak with them without stuttering or looking away. The other day his mother saw him starting fires in the backyard.

"How old is he?" Stanton asked.

"Sixteen."

"I highly doubt it's him. The man we're looking for is probably mid- to late twenties. But I'll still send down an officer to speak with him."

"Please hurry, Detective. I think he's going to really hurt someone."

Stanton stretched his arms and stood up, arching his back as far as it would go before twisting his neck from side-to-side and spinning his arms. It appeared he was limbering stiff muscles, but in reality, he was trying not to fall asleep.

He went around the makeshift call center and listened to everyone's phone calls. Some of them were diligent and actually calling to try to help, many were not. Stanton walked the room once and went for the door to hit the vending machines for a Diet Coke when one of the interns said, "Detective, I think you should hear this."

Stanton turned back to him. The intern put the call on speaker. It was an older woman stating that she had seen the man coming and going from the condominium next door. There was a young woman who lived there, and she never had men over, so it was odd to see him there.

"How old is the young lady?" Stanton asked.

"In her twenties I think. Pretty young thing. She's in pictures, she said."

"Have you ever seen the two of them together?"

"No, he just comes and goes. He may be housesitting because I haven't seen her lately. He looks just like the picture I saw on the news."

Stanton got the address and thanked her for her call. They hung up and Stanton stood quietly for a moment before saying, "I'm running down there myself. Tell Danny where I am when he comes by."

"Sure."

The condominiums were well kept, and most of the cars in the ports were old Cadillacs and Lincolns and Buicks. Easily fifteen or twenty years old, but looking new, freshly cleaned with few dings and scratches. There were colorful flowers next to the common walks, and a few of the windows had American flags hanging from them.

Stanton found the condo he was looking for and parked out front. An elderly couple was up the private road a bit, arguing about something as they made their way to their car. Stanton waited until they had driven away before stepping outside and sitting on the hood of his car, looking around.

When he was satisfied that he couldn't hear anything, he went to the front door of the condo and knocked. He rang the doorbell and put his ear to the door. There was no sound from inside. He walked around out front and noticed that the window leading to the kitchen was broken, and the shattered glass hadn't been cleared away. He pushed through the shrubs and looked through the window. The kitchen was clean except for a few bowls lying out. All the drawers and cupboards were closed. He was about to turn away when he glanced at the floor.

With murder scenes in homes and apartments, most landlords don't tell prospective buyers and renters about the space's history. As they pass by stains on the floors that couldn't be cleaned, most people assume they're from wine or fruit juice. But anyone who saw blood stains enough learned to recognize them. Blood was unique. Blood from veins was bluer and darker than the red arterial blood, and a good homicide detective can tell the difference right away. Stanton knew the small trail of droplets on the kitchen's linoleum floor was of arterial blood, at least a few days old, that no one had bothered to clean up.

He called into dispatch and gave his call number for the homicide unit and requested backup. The nearest unit was at least ten minutes away at another scene. He decided he couldn't wait ten minutes.

Stanton hopped up onto the windowsill and crawled into the home. The window was right above the sink, and he put his palms down on the counters and pulled himself through before jumping onto the kitchen floor. He brushed off the shards of broken glass that had cut up his knees.

He waited quietly until he couldn't hear his heart beating so loudly in his ears. He took out his firearm, a Desert Eagle .45, and held it low as he followed the trail of blood to the carpet of the hallway.

The condo smelled of apple blossoms, a body wash or shampoo a teenage girl might select. A portrait of a family hung on the refrigerator, four young kids and a mother and father at Sea World in front of the walrus exhibit. The mother was making rabbit ears behind the father. Stanton went down the hallway gun first.

Creaking came from upstairs, but not in a way that suggested someone was walking on the floor above him. More as though the floorboards were settling. He scanned the living room. Nothing out of the ordinary and he saw the stairs leading to the second floor. He took them gingerly as he made a slow ascent and heard a groan behind him.

He spun around, his weapon aimed at the origin of the sound coming from the living room, and noticed the bare feet sticking out from near the coffee table. The nails were painted red, and the skin was tanned almost to the point of being orange. He leapt off the stairs and ran to the table, his weapon still in front, as he saw the young woman sprawled on the carpet in between the couch and the coffee table. A white bandage was wrapped around her head, and near the back was a dark red stain on the gauze.

Stanton sat by her and soon heard sirens outside. The girl was only semi-conscious, and a chain bound her to the entertainment center. Stanton didn't remove it. Instead, he held her hand. She looked up at him once and said, "Can I go home now?"

"Yes."

CHAPTER 46

Forensics, Stanton, and Slim Jim ran over the entire condo in the course of several hours. Amber was taken to the emergency room, and Stanton had gotten word that she'd suffered a massive concussion but that she would be all right.

The latent print team had managed to find over twenty-five different sets of prints in the condo. Stanton had them only run the sets found on the windowsill. There were two: one was his, and the other was unidentified. Stanton found a number in his contacts and dialed as he sat down on the couch in the living room.

"Federal Bureau of Investigation, Los Angeles," a female voice said. "How may I direct your call?"

"Mickey Parsons in Behavioral Science, please."

"Who may I say is calling?"

"Jon Stanton with the San Diego Police Department."

"One moment."

There was a long delay and then a click before Mickey's voice came on.

"How are you, Jon?"

"Doing well. I haven't seen you down at the gym in a while."

"Been pretty slammed with paperwork these days."

"I saw the news story about Evonich. That was good work."

"Thanks. I wish we could've snagged him earlier. We searched one of his old homes in Lincoln County, Nebraska, and found the remains of two girls. Sisters. We think there's more, but no one's coming forward with anything else." Stanton heard some papers shuffling. "So I'm guessing this isn't a call just to harass me. What's going on?"

"I have a favor to ask. I was hoping you could run some prints through ViCAP for me."

"No problem, shoot them over."

"I need them as soon as possible. Preferably in the next couple of hours."

"Now that is a favor. Anything I can use to narrow the search? Locales or race?"

"Nothing. We know nothing about him other than a composite sketch we have from witnesses. They say he looked Caucasian, but one of our witnesses saw him from relatively close and thought he might've been of Mediterranean or Middle Eastern descent."

"Well, I'll do what I can. Get me a print card couriered over, and I'll have my guys get on it."

"You're not even going to ask what it's for?"

"I saw you on the news. I thought you might be calling us for something on this one. By the way, you looked like shit."

"Thanks. And I owe you for this."

"Beer and a burger is fine. I'll let you know."

Stanton hung up and put the phone back in his pocket. He rose from the couch and crossed to the entertainment center. There was a rack of DVDs, and he glanced through them. They were mostly Disney and Pixar films with a few romantic comedies thrown in.

"Detective?"

Stanton turned to see one of the forensic techs, a man named Lee Gyun, wiping the sweat off his forehead with the back of his hand.

"Tell me you have something, Lee."

"I have something for you." He held out a small notebook with red leather binding. Stanton slipped on some latex gloves and then took it. "Found it in the bedroom upstairs on the nightstand. Could be our vic's, I don't know, I just flipped through it quickly."

"Thanks."

Stanton began going through the pages. The writings were in pen, and they were so illegible he couldn't make much of them. But there were passages that rang out to him. There were no dates and no times. Many sentences would end without a period, and the next one would start immediately afterward on a completely separate idea. There was no name on the journal, and it was possible that it belonged to the victim or a past victim. On the inside flap of the back cover was an imprint: MSH. On the cover, which was bland and gray, was a number: 1842.

There was one passage toward the front that was fully legible:

they walk through their lives like billboards their clothing has the name of their God corporations on them and they advertise for them as if they are remarking on something of consequence they watch television shows now that feign reality in a way that demeans it they neglect the poor and the weak in favor of the wealthy they are ruled over by a small class of tyrants and they fight for their system as if it would ever give them a fair chance I walked to the store today to feel the air on my face and hear the whisper of the birds but instead only received lungfuls of black exhaust and air that smelled so putrid it made me gag I won't be walking out there again

Stanton flipped through the rest of the journal, reading the legible portions. No names on any page. It was little more than rantings, and some of them had apocalyptic predictions and spoke of cities turned to dust and brothers eating brothers. Stanton finished and set it down on the coffee table. His cell phone buzzed in his pocket and he took it out. It was Childs.

"This is Jon."

"What you got for me?"

"Journal and a set of prints. FBI's running the prints through ViCAP right now."

"What kind of journal?"

"Personal. Still don't know for sure that it's his, but I think so. Nothing to identify him in it."

"Keep me updated."

"How's everything up there?"

"Still running down some leads where we can. The calls are dying out, though. We've only gotten maybe ten the past hour."

"Let me know if there're any good ones."

"Okay." A pause. "Jon, I never doubted you. I want you to know that. That's not why I was riding your ass and took you off this case. There are going to be other cases like this and other vics. I need to know that I can trust you to follow orders. Can I trust you to do that?"

"Yeah, you can trust me."

"Good. Call me if you find anything else."

Stanton hung up and pushed the phone back in his pocket. He couldn't take this anymore. There were no rules to bureaucracy. Even if there were, they were probably corrupt and he wouldn't be able to follow them, anyway. Every day it was as if lead weights were being set on his chest and he couldn't get them off. They would just slowly accumulate until he couldn't breathe anymore and one day would just suffocate him.

This is it. This is going to be my last case.

CHAPTER 47

It was after five by the time Stanton parked in the underground garage and got out of his car to get some sleep. Tomorrow was Sunday, and as much as he wanted to be back at that condo or in the hospital or interviewing the Richardsons, he couldn't. It was the Sabbath, and he fully believed that God had commanded humanity to rest on that day. So Slim Jim had taken over and would be contacting him Monday morning with the results of interviews and anything else they'd found in the condo.

He went inside and sat on his balcony before opening the journal found at the girl's condo. There were passages that seemed to fade in and out of coherence, but sometimes a lucid thought would come through.

A baby screams when born and an old man screams when he dies how can anyone believe that a life that begins this way and ends this way is meant for anything but suffering?

He stared for a long time at the imprint on the back. MSH. They could have been the owner's initials, but the imprint wasn't written in. It was stamped, like an old library card of the type he had in elementary school. He brought his laptop outside on the balcony and Googled "MSH."

Several businesses came up, as did a hormone with "MSH" as its acronym. He brought up a Word document and began typing in a column.

HIGH SCHOOLS OR COLLEGES

FRATERNITIES

BUSINESSES

HOSPITALS

GOVERNMENT AGENCIES

NOVELTY STORES LIKE HALLMARK

There was always the possibility that the owner had simply ordered a stamp with his or her initials, and he couldn't rule that out. But the stamp looked faded and old, and the journal itself was something one would buy in bulk: a plain cover with cheap paper. It didn't strike him as something a person would pick out in a novelty store.

He limited his search to southern California and began searching for high schools with the acronym MSH. He followed through with colleges, universities, and private schools. One school did come up: the Madison Selena Hollinger School for the Blind. He clicked on their website, and copied and pasted the address and phone number into his document.

He moved on to hospitals. The third result from the top caught his interest: the McKay State Hospital of California. Stanton clicked on the link. He went to the ABOUT US tab and read their mission statement. It was a hospital for the criminally insane.

His guts tightened, and an icy feeling ran through his knees and belly, replaced by the warm sensation that came with adrenaline running through his body and heightening his senses. He saved the link to his favorites and did the same on his phone before reading through everything about the hospital. The clock on his laptop said 5:53 p.m. He decided to chance it and called the main line for the hospital.

"McKay," a feminine male voice answered.

"Yes, this is Detective Jon Stanton with the San Diego Police. I'd like to set an appointment to see, hold on… is it a Dr. Nathan

Reynolds?"

"Yeah, he's the administrator. I'm just the night security. I don't set the appointments. But if you come in Monday morning he'll be here. Come in after, like, ten, 'cause he has rounds until nine thirty."

"Thanks. I'll do that."

Stanton hung up. He was about to decide what to do next when his phone rang. It was an unknown number.

"This is Jon Stanton."

"Is this the person who just called the McKay Hospital?"

"Yes."

"And who are you exactly?"

"I'm a detective with San Diego Police. Robbery-Homicide. Who am I speaking with?"

"Just one moment... hmm. I just searched your name and phone number, and it came back accurate. Well, Detective, this is Dr. Reynolds. I was told by night security that you'd called for me."

"Yeah, they told me you wouldn't be in until Monday."

"Saturday nights are my call nights, and I usually just spend them here. I prefer security not let anyone know."

A flash entered Stanton's mind. It was brief, but it encapsulated

Nathan Reynolds's life and gave Stanton a foundation that told him what type of man he was dealing with.

A man who had gone through multiple divorces, women marrying him for his status and realizing that being married to the ego of most physicians was full-time work. He saw a man who drank or gambled or womanized or had some vice that he clung to because he felt it necessary, no matter the cost. Stanton saw loneliness and pain and belief that the time he spent with madness eased that pain. He pictured Nathan Reynolds sitting in a cluttered office with the screams of the insane around him, saying, *At least I'm not them.*

"I'm glad to hear that, Doctor. I had a few questions."

"Certainly."

"I found a journal. It's bland-looking, and the corners are rounded with a rubber coating on them. There's a stamp that says MSH on the inside of the back cover."

"Yes, that's one of ours. We issue journals to our patients for therapeutic purposes."

"This journal was found at the scene of a kidnapping, and we think the owner might be responsible for several homicides." The line went silent, and Stanton noted that the doctor had even stopped breathing. "Doctor? Are you there?"

"Yes. There should be a code on the cover of the journal on the lower left-hand side. A number."

"Yes, it's 1842."

"Just a moment… Detective, I don't think I can release this information without a court order. You will simply have to secure one for me."

"You have a name, don't you? Doctor, this man targets families. He's killed—"

"I know perfectly well what he's capable of, Detective. But I won't be responsible for any HIPAA violations and lose my license. You will have to get a court order."

"Can you tell me at least when he was last incarcerated?"

"We don't incarcerate our patients, Detective," he said, annoyed. "We treat them."

"I apologize. When was he last in for treatment?"

"He was released a little over a month ago."

"May I ask why?"

The doctor exhaled loudly. "There was a woman who worked here. She no longer does. She advocated for his release."

Stanton read exactly what he was saying: the woman, probably a treating psychiatrist, had been sleeping with the man.

"Doctor, without any violations, is there anything else you can tell me?"

"He's extremely intelligent. Once I re-read his file without her sugarcoating it… Look, get the court order, and I'll tell you everything you want to know."

"I'll see you Monday then, with a court order."

"Very well."

Stanton was too wired for sleep. He stood up and paced his apartment and then went back out on the balcony and sat down. He thought about going night surfing as the waves were high, but decided against it. Instead, he lay back and began trying to decipher the entries in the journal.

Stanton woke early on Sunday after having slept only a few hours. The journal entries had filled him with a gray weight that clung to him like heavy glue. He pushed the thoughts out of his mind by going for a jog. He ran the length of the beach in a long circle wearing trail shoes that sank into the sand. He ran for over half an hour before sprinting as long as he could, his breath leaving him, his heart tightening in his chest. Stanton walked for a few minutes and then collapsed on the sand, staring up at the blue, cloudless sky. He sat up, brought his knees to his chest, and watched the waves lap the shore until he had regained enough strength to walk to his apartment.

After a shower and a shave, he went to his nearby church for service.

The pews were not crowded. Outside of Utah, Nevada, and Hawaii, most Mormon churches were not filled to the brim with parishioners. It created a tighter-knit community, as their numbers were limited, but it also meant that each person had more obligations in the church to keep it running smoothly.

Stanton sat in the back, listening to a sermon given by a young woman who was preaching on how to resist temptation when the doors to the church opened and a man stood there. Stanton had never seen him before, but he wore a pressed black suit and a baseball cap and scanned the room as he entered. Stanton turned away and back to the speaker when he saw the man make his way up the aisle and sit next to him.

"You know," the man said loudly, without turning to him, "the thing that's always amazed me about the faithful is that they preach everything in here, but in the real world they're no better than the rest of us. They sleep with prostitutes, and they drink and have abortions. Some of them molest children or beat their wives. So they ask for forgiveness. Forgiveness for things they can't control." He turned to him. "Your Heavenly Father must laugh himself into a coma every day. He issues us passions and then forbids us to give in to them. And these people," he said, motioning with his hand over the pews, "they carry guilt with them and hand it off to their defenseless children. And to top it off, they give money for the privilege of subjecting themselves to this slavery. Religion is quite the racket."

Stanton was about to say something when his pulse began to pound. He knew who the man was. He recognized the sleek jaw line and the eyes that were set just a little too close. Though the hat covered his head, he guessed he was bald underneath.

Stanton's hand slid down to the firearm at his side.

"I wouldn't do that," the man said. "You're going to want to hear what I have to say."

The young lady at the podium closed her talk, and the man stood up and cheered. He whistled and hollered and everyone turned to him. He shouted, "Fucking A!" and sat back down.

"I don't want to spatter your brains in a church," Stanton said. "Come outside quietly, and I'll just arrest you."

He laughed mirthlessly. "How's Emma doing?" Stanton didn't respond, and he kept talking. "She's quite the fighter. When I fuck her I bet she's going to put up—"

Stanton had his throat and pressed him against the pew. The man tried to laugh, but only a low hissing would escape his lips. Stanton pulled out his cell phone and dialed Emma's number. It went straight to voicemail. He dialed again—straight to voicemail.

"What did you do?" Stanton whispered.

The man tried to speak, but nothing would come out as he began to turn red. Stanton let go of the man's throat and sat back, his hand on his firearm.

"She's fine," he said, coughing. "Oh, man. This is fun. I'm glad we did this."

"Tell me where she is."

"I'll do better. I'll take you there. But you can't call anyone. Just me and you. Two buddies."

Stanton shook his head. "No way. I'm hauling you in."

"You'll never find her, and she'll starve to death." He held out his hands as if in surrender. "I don't have weapons. You can keep your gun, I don't care. I promise you, I'll take you to her."

After a couple of moments of thought, Stanton spit out, "Stand up and walk outside. If you run I'll shoot you in the back."

"Spoken like a true disciple of Christ."

The man stood up, and they headed out the double doors. Stanton walked behind him with his hand on the Desert Eagle at his hip. Out in the sunlight in the parking lot, the man took a deep breath and turned to Stanton.

"Let's take your car, Jon. You probably wouldn't trust taking mine. And it's a little bit of a drive."

Stanton removed his firearm and held it low so it wouldn't cause panic. He led him over to his car, and the man got into the passenger seat. Stanton climbed into the driver's seat with the gun held to the man's chest.

"I could shoot you right now, and no one would question me."

"But you won't. I did some reading up on you. Quite the Boy Scout. Sorry about your wife. Is she really marrying someone from the

Chargers? Never liked football. Too much aggression. I think you're the same way, aren't you, Jon?"

"Stop calling me that."

"It's your name, isn't it?"

Stanton struck him with the weapon on the head and pressed the muzzle against his temple, his head pushed against the glass of the passenger side window.

"Did I do something to upset you, Detective?" he said with a chuckle. "It couldn't have been those little kiddies I fried, could it?"

Stanton took out his phone.

"I have to urge you, Detective, not to do that. I will clam up and ask for a lawyer, and she will starve to death. She's somewhere no one ever goes. All I'm asking for is that you take a drive with me out there. After that, I will turn myself in."

"No, you won't."

"I give you my word."

He pulled the gun away from his head. "You don't want to turn yourself in. You want to die."

The man grew quiet. "And you presume too much. Now, are we going to go see Emma or go to the station and let her die?"

Stanton bit his cheek. He transferred the gun to his left hand and pulled out the keys with his right before starting the car.

"I knew you were as smart as you looked, Detective."

They left the church parking lot and took San Bernadisto Drive to the freeway.

"Stay in this lane," the man said. "It'll be about twenty minutes." He leaned back in his seat as if on a leisurely drive. "I read that you almost died and were in the hospital for nearly a month. Your partner, what was his name? Sherman? Or whatever it was. I read it was a fake name, and they still don't know who he is or where he is. He got away pretty free and clear, didn't he?"

Stanton didn't respond.

"Anyway, I was in a hospital for a long time, too. It's an odd place, isn't it? Not quite prison and not quite freedom. You seem to turn in on yourself. Your mind begins to eat itself, like your body does when you don't give it nourishment. I had to read a lot to keep that from happening, but who knows? Maybe it happened and I'm just not aware of it. That's always puzzled me, Detective. I know you have a doctorate in psychology. Tell me, how does one know when one has gone crazy? If you're crazy, you can't tell you're crazy, right?"

Stanton said nothing as a car cut him off and he slowed down.

"Are you really not going to talk to me this whole trip? It would make it quite boring, you know."

"How many?" Stanton said.

"In total? I don't know."

"No, you know. You keep track."

"I used to keep track. But after the first few, you begin to forget things. You would be amazed how mundane killing can get, Jon. How banal. It's like anything else. If you do it enough, it gets boring."

"But you can't stop."

"No, I can't stop. I wouldn't want to. It's still fun. One day it won't be, but right now it is. Do you remember the Zodiac Killer? How they never found him, and they think that he was locked up on other charges or died? I don't think so. People don't consider that murder just started boring him and he moved on to something else. That'll probably happen to me, as well. But you know how that is, you've killed a lot, too."

"Not like you."

"Why? Because you did it for the 'good' of the public? What if someone you had killed, let's say one of the murderers, would've killed someone who was going to kill others down the road. Like, by being a drunk driver? Is that then an evil or good act he's performed? If you measure it by substantive parameters, it was a good act that saved lives. There are too many variables in life, too many unknowns to say what's good and what's evil. Those terms have become outdated."

"When you equivocate good and evil, only good loses out."

He chuckled. "That seems to be the curse of this time, doesn't it? I've been gone years, and coming back I was shocked with what I saw on television, what was considered acceptable behavior. I can see, physically see, that society has become more godless and corrupted. My father predicted it, but I never believed him. He was a preacher—you and he, I think, might've gotten along. Except of course that he raped all the women that surrounded him." He laughed. "I think some of the animals too. Every man has his appetites, I suppose. You're going to want to merge with this interstate."

Stanton swung left, and they followed Interstate 15 for what was easily another half hour. They were in a low-income area, and Stanton could see several government housing projects blotting the landscape. Covered in graffiti, one had an abandoned car in front that had been taken apart.

Getting off the freeway, they drove another few minutes. They came to a line of abandoned homes, and the man pointed to one and said, "Stop in front."

Stanton took out his cell phone. "She's not here," the man said. "You may want to wait before calling it in."

"You said you were taking me to her."

"I am. Be patient, Detective."

He got out of the car, and Stanton followed.

CHAPTER 48

Daniel Childs lifted over three hundred and fifteen pounds on the bench press before sitting up and taking a swig of fruit punch creatine. The gym was packed, and two women in spandex were working out in front of him. He smiled to the one on the right wearing a flower-print tube top, and she smiled back.

He then moved to the preacher curls and did drop-sets until exhaustion. He felt his phone vibrating in his pocket: it was his secretary.

"Yeah, what's up?"

"Internal Affairs is here, Danny. They want to speak with you."

"Well, tell 'em I'm at the gym. They can come back later."

"They said it's urgent. They wanted your cell number, but I told them I would just call you."

"All right, gimme thirty."

Danny saw the young woman glance over at him again. He wanted to go over and speak to her but was short on time. IAD would show up at his house if he didn't meet them at the office. He'd always thought of them as piranhas. Cannibal piranhas. They were necessary to prevent corruption, but the people who were corrupt usually were insulated from them.

He showered and changed into jeans and a zip-up Polo shirt, letting his badge dangle on the chain around his neck. By the time he got to Northern, it was buzzing with activity. He parked out back and went in. Two men in suits sat in his office.

Childs threw his gym bag behind his desk and sat down.

"What do you want, Matt?" he said.

One of the men took out a piece of gum and unwrapped it. "Gum?"

"No, thanks. Now what the fuck do you want?"

"We've gotten some complaints on one of your detectives."

"I'm sure you have. Which detective?"

"Jon Stanton."

"Stanton? What was the complaint?"

"Sexual harassment of a bar manager and assault against one of the bouncers."

Childs chuckled. "Have you seen Jon Stanton? I promise you he couldn't assault no bouncer."

"Well, that's not what his partner said."

"Stephen Gunn told you Stanton assaulted a bouncer?"

"Among other things. We're doing this as a courtesy, Danny. We don't need to alert the supervising officer. He can contact his union rep if he wants and come in with them, but we want some time with him."

"Jon Stanton's the best cop I got. I'd prefer if you sank your teeth into someone else."

"Like who?"

"How about the fucking chief of police? I heard he's got a thing for working girls."

Matt shifted uncomfortably and glanced at his partner. "When Stanton comes back, let us know. We'll be around."

He left one of his cards, and Childs picked it up and tossed it in the trash.

CHAPTER 49

Stanton stood in front of the old house with the pointed roof and considered calling the SWAT team right now, after he'd put a bullet in each of the man's ankles to make sure he was adequately slowed down. But he thought of Emma, tied up in some basement in the dark, slowly starving to death over the coming weeks. The thought caused him pain, physical pain that wrenched his guts. He glanced around and said, "Let's go."

They walked up the path to the house, and the man used a key to get in. The place was empty except for a few beer cans and used hypodermic needles. An old, stained sleeping bag in one corner had developed crisscrossing spider webs. The house smelled like dirt and urine, and Stanton had the urge to snort to get the scent out of his nostrils.

"The basement," the man said.

Stanton followed him to a door. The man opened it and revealed a long set of stairs going down into the dark. He flipped a switch, and a single light bulb came on below, illuminating the way just enough so they might not fall.

The basement was cool and humid. Several cardboard boxes clustered in the center of the room, supporting two monitors hooked up to a laptop. Stanton had difficulty seeing the screens from where he was standing. He lifted his gun to the man's back. "Keep moving," he said.

Coming to the center of the basement, Stanton could see the images clearly now. On one monitor was a family. A male, female, and four children. They were tied at the waist with what looked like some sort of rope, and the children were crying.

On the other screen was Emma. She was tied and gagged.

"What'd you do with her?"

"Guess."

"Tell me where she is, *now*."

"You have a choice. Emma and the family are both surrounded with gallons of napalm. There's a lit fuse working its way around the space at each location. It's got…" He checked his watch. "It's got twenty-five minutes before it reaches the napalm. Each of their addresses are twenty minutes away. One is north, and the other is south. You can only save one of them, Jon."

Stanton grabbed the man and spun him around, bashing his elbow into his face. The man flew off his feet, and Stanton was on him. He struck him once more in the face with his fist and pinned the man down with one hand as he put his firearm on the man's cheek.

"Tell me where she is."

"Fine," he said, laughing as blood poured from his nose, "but then I won't tell you where the family is. Mr. and Mrs. Westfall and their four beautiful children. Too bad, one of the kids was getting straight A's and might've gotten a scholarship to college."

Stanton grabbed the man's collar and lifted him up, dragging him close. "You're going to tell me everything."

"No, I'm not. Here's the real fun part, Jon. If you save the family, you'll never forgive yourself. What if Emma was the one you were supposed to spend your life with, and you let her fry? But if you save Emma, you can never be with her. Your relationship would be tainted. Every time she looked at you it would remind her of me. Eventually, the sight of you would fill her with disgust."

Stanton knew it was true, and it sickened him. He sat up and gripped his Desert Eagle with both hands, steadying them.

"Yes," the man whispered, "do it."

Stanton's hands began to shake.

"Kill me," the man whispered.

Images flashed through his mind, images of the men he had killed in the line of duty. Evil men who couldn't be stopped any other way. It was war, and in war killing was inevitable. It always had been. But this wasn't war. The man was lying helpless on the ground, blood pooling around his head from a broken nose.

"No, I won't kill you," Stanton said.

The man spit a glob of bloody phlegm and wiped his mouth with the back of his sleeve. "You still have to choose. Tick tock tick tock."

Stanton looked at the screens. He saw the faces contorted in pain and anguish. It tore his heart out to see tears streaming down the cheeks of the children and the parents who were helpless to comfort them. Emma was hunched over, defeated. Her hair stuck to her face from tears or blood or both. She looked at the camera and then away. Her eyes were already dead; her hope had been taken from her.

"No," Stanton whispered.

"What?"

"No. I won't choose. I won't play games with you."

"They'll all die, and it's your fault."

"No, it's not. If they die, then they have to die. It's God's will, not mine. But you'll die too. In a gas chamber, with me looking in your eyes through the glass."

"Make a fucking choice," the man spit out.

"No. Turn around and put your hands behind your back."

The man roared in frustration and leapt at Stanton like an animal. He tackled him over the equipment, and they hit the ground hard. Stanton grabbed him by the collar and flipped him over. The man brought up a knee into his groin and then rolled to his stomach, pushing himself up with his arms. Stanton brought the gun up, but the man had already turned around and brought his forearm down against it, sweeping it away and to the floor.

Stanton tried to strike him with an elbow, and the man ducked and took him down to his back again. Stanton wrapped his legs around the man's hips to keep him close so he wouldn't have the leverage to punch. Then he lifted his hips and rolled them. Stanton jumped up but lost his balance and stumbled backward as the man crawled on all fours and grabbed his legs, shoving Stanton to fall back against the wall.

The man was on top of him now and pummeling his face with his fists. He was grunting like a pig as he struck, and the grunts grew louder and turned to screams.

Stanton's face was a pulp of bloody, slick flesh. He felt teeth loose in his mouth and coughed as blood poured down his throat and over his chin. He was dazed and felt a pounding in his head that had nothing to do with the punches but nearly blinded him. He could feel heat in his head just off to the side, where heat shouldn't be. He rolled away.

The man stood up, out of breath, and heard a metal clink as he tried to bring his left hand up. He looked down to see the handcuffs locked on his wrist and on an exposed pipe against the wall.

"No," he screamed, "no no no no no." He began pulling and frenziedly jerking his hand, trying to pull the pipe loose. The flesh on his wrist began to bleed. Realizing it was futile, he jumped at Stanton.

Stanton rolled again but felt the man grab his shoulder. He turned his head back and bit the man's fingers. The man screamed as he let go, and Stanton rolled again, out of reach.

Stanton watched as the man screamed and hollered and pounded the metal pipe with his feet and free hand. He reached down and tried to bite his wrist, not realizing the pain that would result. Stanton grabbed his gun and looked over at the laptop on the floor in the center of the room.

He crawled over, spitting blood in an attempt to keep his mouth clear. The laptop was a blank background image of a green hillside—the desktop. The images of Emma and the family were still on the two monitors. Stanton took out his cell phone and flipped through his contacts before dialing a number.

It rang four times before a male voice answered, "Hello?" He was out of breath, and Stanton could hear a female voice in the background.

"This is Jon. I need you to do something for me," Stanton said, speaking slowly and cautiously, his sibilants slurring from the blood still pooling in his mouth.

"Jon, it's fucking Sunday. I don't work Sundays, man. You got the TV on or something? What's that screaming?"

"I don't have much time, Billy. Please."

He sighed. "Fine, what is it? And stop eating I can barely understand you."

"There're two monitors set up here showing two different live images. They're attached to a laptop. I need to find… I need to find out where the cameras are set up."

"Hm, well, what program's running on the laptop?"

"It's just showing a desktop."

"Any minimized windows?"

Stanton glanced to the bottom of the screen and saw an icon of a flying carpet with a genie on it. "Yes. I opened it. Magic Carpet."

"Oh, yeah, that's easy. On the bottom of the home screen in MC, there should be a settings tab. You see it?"

"Yeah."

"Click on it. Now there should be a locations icon on there. Click that."

"Got it. It's a bunch of numbers."

"It's in longitude and latitude. Just type the numbers into Google Maps, and it'll give you an address."

"I don't know if this has Internet. I need you to do it."

"Can this wait? I got someone here. And what the hell is that screaming, Jon?"

"Do it now," Jon said, and he spit a large glob of blood on the floor. "Or I will come down there and put a bullet through your Mac."

"All right, all right, chill out. What're the numbers?"

Stanton read the numbers. Billy hummed and mumbled something to himself as they came up. He read the addresses off. One was about twenty minutes north. Another was… on this street.

"Thanks," Stanton said.

"No prob but you—"

Stanton hung up and called dispatch. He sent a unit to the address up north and then rose to his feet. He called Slim Jim and told him what was happening. SWAT was called out.

The man was now on the floor, sweat pouring from him as he laughed. "They won't put me in prison. They can't kill me either. I have two Axis One disorders. I'm not competent to stand trial. They'll put me in a state hospital, and I'll get out. And I'm coming to pay you a visit, Jon. Sleep with the lights on."

"I'll be waiting."

Stanton ran up the steps and slipped once, hitting his elbow hard against the step. He got up again and made it outside. The house he was in had the number 2275, and the address he needed was 2304. He ran up the street until he found it. A group of boys across the street eyed him as he ran up the lawn to the door.

It was locked, and Stanton kicked it near the doorknob. It wouldn't open. He fired two rounds into the knob and kicked it again, and this time it broke open. In the living room, hunched over, sat Emma Lyon.

Stanton ran to her. She began to weep as he moved to untie her. Gallons of liquid were set up around her—five containers, in all, with what looked like nylon rope sticking out of their openings. Stanton removed the nylon rope from all of them and followed the rope to another room where a fuse was slowly burning down. He stamped out the fuse and went back to the living room. Emma wasn't there.

He went outside and saw her on the lawn, vomiting, but nothing came up. He knelt beside her as sirens droned in the distance, growing nearer with every second.

CHAPTER 50

Jaime Spencer sat in the dining room booth with her boyfriend

Travis, and they shared a piece of key lime pie with two cups of coffee.

The restaurant was upscale, far more than she was used to, but Travis

had a good income through his contracting business and had pledged

that she wouldn't need to scrape by any longer. The restaurant had

swirling yellow and black lanterns hanging from the ceiling that

matched the lamps on the table. She watched the movement as Travis

spoke with the waiter.

"What are you thinking about?" he asked when the waiter left.

"I can't wait to move. I've lived in California all my life." She

looked out the large windows at the beach that was less than twenty

feet away from the restaurant's entrance. "I've never even left the state.

Did I tell you that?"

He took a sip of his beer. "No, but you're a woman full of

mysteries. That's why I'm crazy about you."

She smiled and rubbed his hand. Jaime had been feeling a sense of contentment that she hadn't felt in decades. It was calming, and it began in her belly and moved up in warm waves over her face and down her arms to the tips of her fingers. She had been striving for something her whole life, trying to find something. She had never been able to define what exactly she was looking for or why she needed it. Now she felt the urge wasn't as powerful. She hadn't found what she had been looking for. Somehow she knew that, but at least it wasn't consuming her. And Travis was a decent man, an honest man in a legitimate business. Sure, he was much older than she was, but that hadn't really been an issue so far.

"I have to run to the ladies room."

She rose and gave Travis a kiss on the forehead as she headed past the booths and down a hallway to the women's restroom. She glanced under the stalls to make sure she was alone. She took the small vial of cocaine out of her purse and tipped it against her wrist, pouring a small line, and snorted with one nostril. It felt silky going up. It was pure and nearly uncut.

Jaime wiped her nose and went back to the restaurant. She walked down the hallway and turned toward the booth and saw a man sitting across from Travis, speaking with him. She thought it might have been a friend of his, and then she saw the prominent nose set against the large boxer's cheekbones.

Stephen Gunn looked up at her and smiled. "Hi, Jaime. How are ya? I was just talkin' to Travis here. Seems you never mentioned me. Must've slipped your mind, huh?"

She glanced up at the door, thoughts racing through her mind.

"Have a seat," he said. She didn't move. "Jaime," he said forcefully, "have a seat."

She gripped the edge of the table and sat down next to Travis. Gunn was smiling as he picked up her coffee cup, sniffed, and took a sip.

"I didn't think I'd see you here," Jaime said as casually as possible.

"Because you thought I was dead, right?"

She cleared her throat, her face turning red as Travis glared at her.

"Listen," Travis said, "I don't know who the hell you are or—"

"You wanna tell him, Jaime? Tell him who the hell I am. What's the matter? Cat got your tongue?"

She put her hands on the table and noticed that they were trembling. "I don't know what you think you've heard, Stephen, but it's not true."

"Really? Travis here was just tellin' me you got two one-way tickets to Seattle. Ain't that right, Travis? Now, why would you be movin' to Seattle, I wonder?"

"What are you going to do?" Jaime said nervously.

"You set me up, you whore."

"Hey," Travis said. "You can't—"

"Shut the fuck up, old man. This doesn't concern you."

"He has nothing to do with this," she said. Travis tried to say something, but Jaime stopped him by placing her hand on his shoulder. "What are you going to do with me?" she said to Gunn without looking at him.

"Come outside."

Gunn rose, and Jaime could see the 9mm in his holster. She stood, telling Travis to wait for her, and followed him out of the restaurant into the noonday sun. Gunn was limping and had a cane, but other than that he appeared in good health.

"Did you think those crackheads could take me out?"

"It wasn't me. I had nothing to do with that."

Jaime felt the sting of the back of Gunn's hand across her cheek.

"Don't fuckin' lie to me!" he shouted.

Fear and panic gripped her. Normally, she was smooth and used her sexuality as a weapon. She had never needed to carry a gun for that very reason. But now, as she stared at the fury in his eyes, she knew there was nothing she could say. He was going to kill her.

She turned and ran, Gunn shouting behind her. She glanced back to see him pull his firearm out. As she turned back around, she hit something, and her head snapped up. Jon Stanton stood on the beach, his arms on her shoulders as Gunn limped over through the sand.

"This don't got nothin' to do with you, Jon."

"Put your gun away, Stephen."

"That whore set me up."

Jaime, terror choking her, managed to spit out, "You rape me, you beat me, you take over my house. I can't even sleep at night because I think my door's gonna open and you're going to rape me in my sleep."

"Rape you? When have I ever fuckin' raped you? You're a damn whore. You fuck people, that's what you do."

"Stephen," Stanton said calmly, "put the gun away."

Gunn didn't move, the 9mm hanging limply at his side. Stanton pulled out his Desert Eagle.

"You kiddin' me?" Gunn said. "You gonna pop me?"

"I don't want to do this. But I won't let you kill her."

"She tried to have me shot, Jon."

"I know. And you should've told me and had her arrested. This isn't the way it works."

"Oh, fuck you. I am so sick of your sanctimonious bullshit. You think you're so high and mighty? You think your Jesus looks down on you, happy at what you've turned out to be? How many men you killed, Jon? How many widows are out there 'cause of you? What kinda man kills that many people and thinks he can lecture others about what's moral?"

"A flawed one. That's all I am, Stephen. A flawed man trying to be good. I don't want to do this. Put your gun away."

Gunn didn't move, but his lower lip curled. Then he tucked the gun back into its holster. "We're through, you and me," he said.

As Gunn stormed away, Stanton turned to Jaime. She was going to say thank you, but something didn't fit. Something was off, and she didn't feel it would be appropriate. But he didn't wait for her to say it anyway. He replaced the gun in its holster and turned away from her without saying a word. He walked to the edge of the beach where the water was breaking on the shore and took something out of his pocket.

It shone in the sunlight, and she guessed it was a badge.

He cocked his arm back and flung it into the ocean as far as it would go. It flew through the air and landed with a small splash. Stanton turned from it, looked once at her, and then walked away, off the beach.

EPILOGUE

Emma sat at a booth by the window of the small café. It was sunny out, and the weather appeared calm in a cloudless sky. She sipped coffee and read on her tablet. The waiter came by a couple of times, but she told him she was waiting for someone. She looked out at the street and watched the cars as they passed by, looking at the faces of the drivers. When she was young, she had played a game where she would try to guess what they did for a living or where they were going. If they had a wife or husband waiting for them somewhere.

When she grew older, she began guessing how they would die. She stopped playing the game after that.

She saw the front entrance open, and Jon Stanton walked in. He was wearing shorts and a T-shirt with sandals and appeared far tanner than even a week ago. He came to her table with a smile and sat down across from her, picking up a menu without saying anything.

"How was surfing?" she asked.

"Fine. The waves were good, and there wasn't any wind. I'll have to take you as soon as you're ready."

"I'd like that."

The waiter came back, and Stanton ordered a fish sandwich with fries and a Diet Coke. He reached across the table and held Emma's hand as he looked out the window at the sky. Emma studied his face. When they had first met, she noticed that he would crinkle his brow in a look of concentration. The look seemed permanent, as he would sometimes have it even when he was relaxing. It was gone now.

She thought he had never looked happier.

"We should go somewhere," he said. "Just go to the airport and get on the first plane we find. No matter where it's going."

She smiled and ran her finger over a scar he had on the back of his hand. "I'd like that."

He leaned over the table and kissed her.